"So maybe I ha[...] that's technical[...] spontaneous. Big deal. It doesn't mean that I'm a prude or anything."

"Alright. If you say so."

"It doesn't," she insisted.

He shrugged his shoulders and started to walk off.

Suddenly hit with a burst of inspiration, Sofia grabbed Ram by his hand and pulled him back. When he turned back, laughing, she cupped both sides of his face and laid a kiss on him that was so powerful he couldn't help but let out a grunt of pleasure. He raked one hand through her thick hair and settled the other against the small of her back.

Ram couldn't believe how sweet she tasted or how soft her small curves were. Was this a dream?

Sofia pulled her lips back all too soon but he chased after them for another intoxicating dose. It only lasted for a few extra seconds before she pushed back.

"There," she whispered, while gulping in air. "Is that spontaneous enough for you?"

Before he could answer, she stepped past him on wobbly knees and quickly rushed toward her room before she spontaneously ripped his clothes off.

Behind her, Ram watched her go with a widening smile. Things were finally moving in the right direction.

Books by Adrianne Byrd

Kimani Romance

She's My Baby
When Valentines Collide
To Love a Stranger
Two Grooms and a Wedding
Her Lover's Legacy
Sinful Chocolate
Tender to His Touch
Body Heat
Lovers Premiere

Kimani Arabesque

When You Were Mine
Finding the Right Key
Wishing on a Star
Blue Skies
Feel the Fire
Defenseless
Controversy
Forget Me Not
Love Takes Time
Queen of His Heart

ADRIANNE BYRD

is a national bestselling author who has always preferred to live within the realms of her imagination, where all the men are gorgeous and the women are worth whatever trouble they manage to get into. As an army brat, she traveled throughout Europe and learned to appreciate and value different cultures. Now she calls Georgia home.

Ms. Byrd has been featured in many national publications, including *Today's Black Woman, Upscale* and *Heart and Soul.* She has also won local awards for screenwriting.

In 2006 Adrianne Byrd forged into the world of Street Lit as De'nesha Diamond. In 2008 she jumped into the young-adult arena writing as A. J. Byrd, and she is just hitting the women's fiction scene as Layla Jordan. She plans to continue creating characters that make people smile, laugh and fall in love.

ADRIANNE BYRD

Lovers Premiere

KIMANI™
ROMANCE

This book is dedicated to A.C. Arthur,
Ann Christopher and Brenda Jackson.
It was a pleasure working with you talented ladies.

KIMANI PRESS™

ISBN-13: 978-0-373-86184-2

LOVERS PREMIERE

Copyright © 2010 by Harlequin Books S.A.

www.kimanipress.com

Printed in U.S.A.

Dear Reader,

It's time to step back into the Limelight! *Lovers Premiere* is the final book in this passionate, glamorous Hollywood series, and this time around we are getting the scoop on Sofia Wellesley and Ramell "Ram" Jordan. Ram's had a crush on Sofia since they were both just kids, but the journey to love can be full of obstacles, and somewhere along the way they became the worst of enemies. When a business assignment forces Sofia and Ram to work together, it will cause them to reevaluate just what they mean to each other. And it will become difficult to deny the passion that's been steadily building between them.

The sensuality meter has been turned all the way up in this sizzling story, and the couple's romance brings the Love in the Limelight series to a scorching close. So sit back, relax and enjoy the show!

Be sure to look for my Kimani Romance novel *My Only Desire* in April 2011.

Wishing you the best of love,

Adrianne

Prologue

"Sofia Wellesley, will you marry me?"

Ten-year-old Sofia's amber-brown eyes sparkled at the bundle of wild daisies Ramell Jordan thrust toward her. Daisies were her favorite flower and always put an instant smile on her face—which he knew very well. As for his ridiculous question, she just rolled her eyes and pretended not to have heard it.

"For me? Thank you." She took the flowers and shoved them under her nose so she could inhale their fresh spring scent.

Ram waited and then his wide smile crumbled into a frown when his girlfriend walked away. "Aren't you going to answer my question?" he asked, as they strolled through the back gardens of the Wellesley Estate.

"What question is that?" she asked absentmindedly, still drifting away from him in her bubble-gum-pink sundress.

"C'mon. You know." He stopped following her and folded his arms under his chest. "I've only been asking you every day for the last two weeks."

Sofia kept walking and smelling her flowers. About a minute later, Ram ran and caught up with her just like she knew he would.

"Well?" he tried again.

"I told you that I needed to think about it. Marriage is a very important decision in a girl's life and it's not something to be taken lightly," she said, quoting her mother perfectly. "And just because I've known you all my life doesn't mean that we're destined to be together. We may grow up and want to see other people."

Ram frowned. He didn't like the sound of that. "See other people like who?"

Sofia shrugged her thin shoulders. "I don't know. There's like a gazillion people in the world."

"You want to date a gazillion people?" he asked with his eyes practically bugging out. "Do you have any idea how long that would take?"

"I don't know. Probably like five years."

"Well, five years is a looooong time."

Finally, she stopped walking and turned toward him. "Momma said that if a boy really liked you then he would wait, no matter how long it takes."

Ram tossed up his hands. "That's ridiculous! What am I supposed to do while you're out dating a gazillion people—play Atari and drink juice boxes?"

"Oh stop being overly dramatic." Sofia rolled her eyes. "You're going to do what all boys do: work and save a lot of money."

"Wait a minute. I work while you date other people? That hardly seems fair."

"Oh, I'll work too," she said, beaming. "I'm going to work with my dad and Uncle Jacob. I'm going to work with movie stars, directors, writers—you name it."

"You're going to do all that *and* date a gazillion people?" He rolled his eyes and then shook his head. "All of that is going to take forever. We'll be *old*—like thirty or thirty-five."

Sofia's brows stretched upward. "Are you saying that you won't want to marry me when I'm old?"

"What? No. I didn't say that," Ram backtracked. "I'm just saying that I want to marry you while you're young, too."

"Well we're young now. And we see each other every day as it is so what's the problem?"

"I didn't think we had a problem until you said you wanted to date a gazillion people. If you can lower that number down some then maybe…"

"Okay. How about a bazillion?"

He crossed his arms and gave her a stern look. "Lower."

"A billion."

"Lower."

"A million."

"Lower."

"Umm…a thousand?"

Ram shook his head. "No."

"Lower than a thousand?"

"Definitely."

"A hundred."

"Lower."

"Fifty."

He paused as if it was a number he could work with but then started shaking his head. "Lower."

"Oh, I give up. You're being totally unreasonable." Sofia turned and stormed toward the sprawling mansion.

"Fine. If you're going to start dating other boys then I'm going to start dating other girls—starting with Twyla Henderson."

Sofia stopped in her tracks and turned around. "What did you just say?"

Pleased to see that he'd finally gotten her attention, Ram thrust his chin up and puffed his chest out. "You heard me. I'm going to date Twyla Henderson. She's pretty enough and I know for a fact that she likes me."

"And you also know very well that I don't like that big bully. All she does is talk bad about people and think that everyone should kiss her butt because her father knows a bunch of famous people."

"Whatever. She's always nice to me." Ram turned and started to stroll in the opposite direction, mimicking one of Sofia's slick moves. He smiled when he heard her stomping up behind him.

"Ramell Jordan, I *forbid* you to go out with that knock-kneed cow."

He turned around, laughing. "Knocked-kneed?"

"You heard me." She pushed up her chin. Her anger made red splotches on her smooth brown skin.

"I don't know." He shook his head. "Hardly seems fair that you can date millions of people but I can't see *one* girl that goes to our school."

"You can date anybody but her!"

"Okay. How about Jill Marshall?"

Sofia's face twisted in disgust. "The girl that makes bubbles in her milk every day at lunch? Why would you want to go out with her?"

"Connie Woods?"

Sofia opened her mouth but then closed it. She liked Connie. Everybody did. When she hesitated, Ram took her silence as a stamp of approval.

"Great! I'll go over to her house right now. Maybe she'd like to go to the arcade or the roller rink." He started to march off.

"Ramell Jordan, you'll do no such thing!"

He had her now, but he quickly fixed his face so that he looked confused. "Why not?"

"Because I forbid it," she said, as if it made all the sense in the world.

A smile ballooned across his face. "Admit it. You don't like the idea of me dating other girls just like I don't like the idea of you dating a *gazillion* boys."

Sofia pressed her lips together like she wasn't about to admit to any such thing.

Seeing that she was going to continue to be stubborn about the issue, Ram shrugged his shoulders and said, "Fine. I guess I'll go see what Connie is doing."

He took one step forward and Sofia grabbed his wrist so fast that she dropped half of her fresh-picked daisies. "Don't go!"

Ramell cocked his head and waited for the words he wanted to hear.

"All right. Fine." She snatched her hand back and folded it across her chest with her other one. "I don't want you to date other girls. There. Are you happy?"

"Extremely." He turned toward her. "So how about getting married?"

"Sofia! Dinnertime! Time to come in!" Gloria, the Wellesleys' housekeeper, hollered out through the French doors.

Sofia's face split into a smile. "See you tomorrow!" She turned and shot off toward the house.

"Wait!" Ram called after her, but it was no use. She was already running as fast as her long legs could carry her.

He crossed his arms dejectedly. "Women!"

Sofia raced into the house, laughing because she had managed to get away from Ram once again without having to answer his proposal. Of course their game would resume tomorrow and she'd have to come up with a whole new set of stall-tactics. Heaven knows that she wasn't opposed to marrying Ramell. The two times that he'd managed to sneak a kiss from her from underneath the oak tree in her backyard she actually thought it was rather nice. Sofia liked Ram. She especially liked how his dark brown eyes would shine like two new marbles when she'd let him. But they were only ten years old. What was a girl to do?

"Go on and wash up," Gloria said, pulling her from her reverie. "Your parents are busy with something in your father's study, but when they're done they'll join you and your sister in the dining room."

Sofia nodded and then ran through the house and up the long spiral staircase to her bedroom. Once inside, she hurried over to the pink vase on top of her chest of drawers and added the four remaining wild daisies she clutched in her hand with the other ones Ram had given her this week. It was starting to look like one of the huge bouquets her father usually sent her mother.

"Mrs. Sofia Jordan," she practiced saying the name a few times in the mirror. "Mrs. Ramell and Sofia Jordan." It had a nice ring to it, she decided. After standing there and admiring her wildflowers for a minute, she sighed and then turned toward her adjoining bathroom to go wash her hands for dinner. On her way back down the hallway, she stopped by her sister's bedroom to peek inside.

A year ago, when her parents first brought Rachel home, Sofia was absolutely not in favor of the whole kid-sister idea. But the moment her mother had put Rachel into her arms for her to hold for the first time, things changed. Sofia didn't expect the new baby to be so cute and adorable. It was love at first sight. She knew from that moment on that she would be like a second mom to her sister. And so far, that's exactly what she turned out to be.

Seeing that Rachel was still fast asleep, Sofia carefully tiptoed backwards and continued to head back downstairs. However, she hadn't even reached the middle stair before a tide of angry voices rose from her father's study. If she had been told once, she had been told a million times not to go into her father's study when the door was closed. But given the amount of yelling that was going on, her curiosity took over and the next thing she knew she was creeping into the room.

As she poked her head in, the first thing she noticed was her father's handsome face distorted and inflamed with anger.

"You think that I don't know what the hell is going on in my own house?"

"John, John. Calm down," Uncle Jacob, her father's twin, tried to pull him away from Emmett Jordan.

"No, Jacob. Wait until you hear about this…this low-life son-of-"

"JOHN," Sofia's mother yelled.

"This *backstabber*," he yelled, "has been sneaking around here with my own wife!" His narrowed gaze shifted to his wife. "Isn't that right, Vivian?"

"No, John!"

"Don't lie to me!" He charged toward her, but once again Uncle Jacob jumped in and blocked his path.

Vivian gasped and stepped back.

"I know what's going on! I've seen you two with my own eyes!"

Her mother dropped her head into her hands and sobbed.

Her father's rampage continued. "Fine! You want

her…you can have her. But it'll be a cold day in hell before I let you take my children and my company away from me!"

"John, please," Sofia's mother wailed.

Uncle Jacob kept his hold around his brother. "Everybody just needs to calm down."

"Calm down?" John questioned wildly as he twisted his way out of his brother's arms. "You know what? *Everybody get the hell out of my house!"*

A hand landed on Sofia's shoulders and she nearly jumped ten feet into the air.

"What are you doing in here?" Gloria hissed.

"I was just…I was…"

"Sofia?" Vivian Wellesley turned her stunned, tear-stained eyes toward her and the housekeeper. "Get her out of here!"

"Yes, ma'am." Gloria grabbed Sofia's arm and dragged her out of the study and shut the door.

"What's going on, Gloria?" Sofia asked with panic settling in her bones. She'd never seen her father so angry before.

"Don't worry about it," the housekeeper said, escorting her to the dining room. "That's grown folks business. None of that concerns you."

Doesn't concern me? Her father had just yelled at her mother and Ramell's father for sneaking around and then accused him of trying to steal his company—a company that he and Uncle Jacob had poured blood, sweat, and tears into. Everyone knew how much her father worked and loved that company. And her mother…how could she?

Sofia plopped down at the dinner table and folded her arms in a huff. She knew how. Emmett Jordan was every bit as much of a charmer as his son, Ramell. Clearly, neither one of them could ever be trusted.

Ever.

And that belief would be held for a long time, because Sofia's parents were killed in a plane crash two days later.

Chapter 1

Los Angeles, Today

Sofia sat on the edge of the doctor's table with her cell phone tucked between her shoulder and her ear while her fingers raced across her iPad as she fired off one contract counteroffer after another.

"Sorry, Larry, but that's not going to happen. You've only locked down Ethan Chambers for two seasons of *Paging the Doctor.* And you got off cheap, if you ask me. If you want to get him on board for another four years then you're going to have come up with a figure that doesn't insult my intelligence."

She only half listened to Larry Franklin's response because she knew that this was the part when studios start crying broke or downplaying just how important her client is to their hit shows. But in this case, it would all be irrelevant because Ethan Chambers dominated the tabloids and magazine covers—despite the mild hiccup with him, her sister and the paparazzi a couple of months ago.

"Larry, if you feel that way then we can just let the contract run out and I can dedicate more attention to the numerous *movie* offers that have been flooding my inbox. You know Denzel Washington started off on a medical show and then exploded on the big screen. That just might be the way to go here. Ethan has the looks and the talent, after all."

"Damn, Sofia. You're really going to bust my balls over this."

That managed to put a smile on her face. "I don't have any idea what you're talking about."

"I'm sure you don't." He laughed. "Just like I'm sure this hard bargain you're driving has nothing to do with Ethan Chambers being in queue to become your brother-in-law."

"You're right. I fight for all my clients."

"Duly noted. I'll get back with you with a counter-offer."

"I'll be waiting," Sofia sing-songed before disconnecting the call. But as soon as she had her phone started ringing again. She was about to answer when Dr. Turner's bored baritone startled her.

"You think you can fit in time for your checkup?"

Sofia nearly jumped and flashed him with an apologetic smile. "Sorry about that, Brian." She quickly put her phone on vibrate and sat it and her iPad down.

"How long do I have before you pick that up again?" he asked, flipping open her chart.

"Two minutes," she answered honestly. Her addiction to her gadgets was well known and quite frankly *not* a laughing matter.

Her longtime friend and doctor shook his head. "I said it before and I'll say it again. You work too much, Sofia."

"Don't be ridiculous. When you love what you do then it's not considered work."

Still shaking his head, Dr. Turner reached for the blood pressure cuff and wrapped it around her arm. "When was the last time you had a vacation?"

Exhaling, Sofia rolled her eyes while she tried to recall the date. "Honey, I don't know. A couple of years ago, I think." She reached over to take a peek at her vibrating phone.

"Let it go to voicemail," the doctor ordered while pumping air into the cuff.

She withdrew her hand from the phone and tried to pretend that she wasn't about to look at it.

"Not good," he said, listening through the stethoscope and watching the needle on the cuff.

"What?" Sofia looked down as if she could decipher the numbers he was reading.

"Your blood pressure is up...*again*." He pulled the cuff off of her arm and leveled her with a stern look. "Look, Sofia. I'm talking to you as both your doctor *and* your friend. You have to do better about controlling all this stress. You keep going down this road and you're going to have a meltdown."

"Ugh." She fought hard not roll her eyes. If she had a nickel for every time someone told her that—mainly her Uncle Jacob—she'd be...well, she was already rich, but she would Bill Gates rich.

"I'm serious, Sofia. You need to cut your stress levels," Brian warned, pulling out his prescription pad.

"What are you doing?" Sofia asked when he started scribbling.

"What does it look like? I'm putting you on medication."

"Great. Then what's the problem? I just pop a pill and everything is cool." She picked up her phone and Dr. Turner quickly took it out her hands.

"No. You don't just pop a pill. You still need to try and slow down, watch what you eat and what you drink or you're going to go down the same destructive path that all workaholics go down that leads to an early grave." He handed over her prescription.

Sofia frowned at his scare tactics. "Will that be all?"

"How's your love life? Are you seeing anyone?"

"What the hell does that have to do with the price of tea in China?"

"I'm going to take that as a no." He folds his arms. "You need to get out. Relax. Get a life. Meet someone."

"Limelight is my life. It's all I need."

Thirty minutes later, Sofia strolled into Limelight Entertainment Management while switching back and forth between two different business calls on her Bluetooth. Still, she flashed smiles to staffers while she continued to chew studio executives and directors out without missing a beat.

"Mrs. Wellesley, your uncle wants to see you in the conference room," Sarah Cole, perhaps the best assistant in the world, whispered to her. "He said to direct you there as soon as you walk into the door."

Sofia just smiled and ignored the order by continuing her march toward her office. Her Uncle Jacob was the last person she wanted to talk to. His little stunt to merge their *family* company with Artist Factory, Inc.— Emmett and Ramell Jordan's company—despite her numerous verbal protests, was a slap in the face that she just couldn't ignore or bring herself to forgive him for anytime soon.

But when she entered her office, she stopped short upon seeing her uncle sitting on her office couch.

"Larry, something just came up. I'm going to have to call you back." She tapped her ear once. "Frasier, I have to call you back." She pulled the gadget from her ear and made a beeline toward her desk. "What are you doing in here?"

"I came to see you since I knew that you wouldn't come to the conference room like I requested."

"I'm busy, Uncle Jacob. What is it?" She asked absently as she plopped into her seat and turned to face her computer.

Jacob heaved himself up from the couch and strolled toward her desk. "First things first. How was your doctor's visit?"

She cut a look toward him as if to ask *are you serious?*

Still he stood there waiting so she answered with a slight lie. "Fine."

His brows lifted slowly until they stretched to the center of his forehead. "So I look like an idiot now? The shakes, the occasional vertigo and chest pain is all normal for a *healthy* thirty-five year old woman?"

Sofia gasped. "Allegedly thirty-five." She glanced around him to double-check that they were alone in the room together. Then she said quietly, through clenched teeth, "A woman, especially in this town, never reveals her age."

"Come on, Sofia. It isn't really your age we're talking about anyway. Tell me the truth."

"Fine. Dr. Turner said something about my blood pressure being *slightly* elevated. He gave me a prescription. It's no big deal." She glanced at her watch. "Now if we're finished discussing my health, I have a ton of calls to get through today."

"They can wait. We need to discuss details about this merger with A.F.I. I've been calling your assistant for weeks now to book a joint meeting with all the parties involved so this transition can go smoothly, but the one person I can't seem to get on the phone is you."

Sofia tossed her hands up in the air. "I don't know what you need my help for. You certainly didn't want to listen to me when I told you that I thought that this merger was a big mistake. Apparently my opinion doesn't matter around here despite supposedly being second-in-command."

Jacob sucked in a frustrated breath. "I'm not going

to keep going around and around with you on this. This merger is a done deal. I know in my heart that this would've been something that even your father would've approved of."

"Like hell he would have."

"Sofia!"

"What? I'm just being honest here. You used to appreciate my honesty. Has that changed, too? Just let me know and I'll just keep my mouth shut."

Jacob slammed his hand on her desk. "How about you just keep the attitude?"

Stunned, Sofia was momentarily unable to respond.

"Now I appreciate and respect your opinion on this matter, but *I'm* still president of this company, and our merging with A.F.I. makes sound financial sense. Plus, Ramell can go a long way in helping to lighten your load around here and you need to take advantage of it."

"I *don't* need Ramell Jordan's help with anything."

"Use him anyway. In fact, I'm ordering you to delegate some of your workload to him. No more ninety-plus hour work weeks, Sofia. You need to start taking better care of yourself."

Sofia opened her mouth to protest, but her uncle cut her off.

"You fight me on this then I'll have no choice but to fire you."

"What?"

"You heard me. Since you're too hardheaded to take care of yourself then it looks like I'm going to have to force you to do it."

With her mouth still hanging open, he turned and started to march out the door.

"By the way, Ramell Jordan is waiting for you in the conference room. You have five minutes to get in there."

Chapter 2

Ramell glanced at his watch and then resumed pacing back and forth in the conference room. He was more than a little annoyed about wasting a whole hour to meet with Sofia to discuss the transition between the two companies. This was a power move, plain and simple. He knew Sofia well and he knew that she was still fighting this merger tooth and nail.

He, like her Uncle Jacob, saw the financial advantage in merging their two companies together. Together they would be able to give some of the big-name agencies some real competition in this town. When his father and the Wellesleys started their family agencies back in the day they were more like boutique operations serving a niche market for African-American actors. For Limelight, it was Sofia who expanded their clientele to include other artists in the entertainment field, but now it was time to expand their scope to include all actors, musicians, models and directors, no matter their race, in order to compete in today's mainstream market.

On top of that, merging their Los Angeles and New York offices would also free up capital to open new offices in Paris and London. As far as Ramell was concerned this was a no-brainer. Sofia—not so much. In fact, the only thing she'd said to everything proposed so far was a steadfast *no*. Limelight was a family company and she wanted to keep it that way. End of story.

By now he shouldn't be surprised. He'd been running into the same brick wall with Sofia for the past twenty-five years. He would've thought by now that he would be used to the pain, but he wasn't. The main reason being that he was still in love with Sofia, despite the fact that she made it clear that she couldn't stand to be in the same room with him.

The reason? That was one thing he didn't know. One day they were best friends, talking in her backyard about marriage, and the next she was avoiding him like the plague. Thinking she was just playing games again, he'd gone through with his promise to date Connie Woods, only for it not to faze her. Or if it did, she sure as hell didn't let it show.

Before he could get to the bottom of it, John and Vivian Wellesley were killed in a plane crash. They were flying into Aspen, Colorado, on their private jet. Their death sent a shockwave through the Black Hollywood community and even caught the attention of the rabid mainstream paparazzi.

The whole thing came as a shock to the Jordan family,

as well. Ram remembered his father being distraught over the whole incident because there had been some kind of falling out a couple of days before their death. Ramell tried to get to the bottom of what happened but whenever he tried to discuss the matter, his father would clam up, even to this day, which was odd considering how close he was to his father. If Ram didn't know any better, he would've sworn that his father blamed himself for what went down and that just didn't make any sense.

Regardless, he thought that eventually the whole situation would settle down after some time had passed and Sofia and her sister Rachel moved in with her aunt and uncle. That never happened. Whatever the story was, Ram suspected that Sofia knew what really happened and she was equally determined to keep him in the dark as everyone else.

Still, his love for her remained true. If anything it only grew. From a distance Ram watched as Sofia transformed from a pretty young girl into a gorgeous woman. A tall, willowy woman who looked more like the models that graced glossy fashion magazines than a woman who represented them. Sofia stunned everyone who met her because she was as smart as she was beautiful.

The only balm for his broken heart was the fact that he hadn't been forced to watch her settle down with another man and bear a house load of children. He didn't know whether he could survive something like that. Still, he did have to watch her turn herself into a workaholic in order to carry on what she perceived as her father's dream. Of course, that was a little bit like the pot calling the kettle black since Ram also put in long hours since he took control of A.F.I. But he still managed to squeeze in *some* time off and even the occasional vacation.

Sofia did not. She lived and breathed Limelight. It was her husband, her children—her life.

"I'm sorry to have kept you waiting," Sofia said, breezing into the conference room and not even bothering to glance in his direction.

Ram's head swiveled toward the tall hurricane that just blew into the room. His eyes immediately landed on her long, cinnamon-brown legs streaming from a short dark blue mini skirt. He quickly placed a hand over his mouth as if he just had a thought, but in truth it was just a sly way to do a hidden drool check. As Sofia dropped down into a chair, Ram's gaze was forced to take in her small waist, her flat stomach and her in-your-face D-size breasts that if he didn't know any better would swear they were calling his name. Just her being in the room erased his previous annoyance, but it didn't mean that he was just going to let her blatant lie slip past him.

"Somehow I doubt inconveniencing me troubles you in the slightest," he said, returning to his chair.

She smiled as if to validate his assessment. "Let's just get down to business, shall we?" She flipped open a fat folder and started reading the contents as if it was the first time she'd seen the documents. He doubted that, since it was well known that she went over everything with a fine tooth comb. But while she pretended to be engrossed with what was written on the page, Ram took a brief moment to mentally photograph her flawless face. Her long lashes looked like two perfect black fans and her strong cheekbones and long flowing black hair hinted at the American-Indian heritage that was buried somewhere in her family tree. He could sit there for the rest of the day admiring individual parts of her just as he could sit back and appreciate the entire package. Most of the time, he liked to do as much of both as he could.

Sofia drew a deep breath. "I guess the best way to tackle this is to decide who is ultimately in charge of which department in order to avoid overlap in duties."

"Actually, Jacob and I have already discussed that part. I was under the impression that you were bringing me some of your client files to this meeting."

Sofia's head snapped up. "Excuse me?"

Hit with the full force of her beautiful brown eyes, Ram sucked in a long breath. It was already bad enough that he had to sit there and pretend that her Marc Jacobs perfume wasn't working a number on his senses, but to pretend like those eyes, those cheekbones and that beautiful, full mouth wasn't causing his pants to fit a little tighter in the inseam would require better acting chops than he possessed. He coughed and then pulled his gaze away from her. "I came here to help lighten your load. Jacob said—"

"I'm not about to turn over my clients to you. Are you crazy?"

Ram blinked and stared back at Sofia silently for a moment.

"Do you know how *long* it took me to develop my list? Do you have any idea how much work it involved to develop a rapport with my clients and studio heads?"

"I think I have some idea, yes." Ram shook his head. "You know it's not my first time to the rodeo here," he said with a laugh, trying to lighten the mood. It didn't work.

Sofia leaned back in her chair and calmly folded her arms beneath her very lovely breasts and said simply, "No."

Ram forced his gaze up from her creamy brown cleavage peeking through her white top and met her steady gaze again. "No?"

"Good. We understand each other." She slapped her folder shut and jumped up from her chair. "Now that we got all that settled, I have some work to do." She flashed him a frosty smile and attempted to leave.

"Whoa, whoa, whoa." Ram instantly popped up and snaked a hand out to grab her by her wrist.

Sofa stiffened while her gaze dropped down to his offending hand.

Without her saying a word, he got the picture and released her. "Sorry."

She turned and squared off. "Look. Let's get something straight. I'm against this merger."

"Clearly."

"And I think the way you and Jacob went about this was sneaky and underhanded. And since you and my uncle cooked this whole thing up behind my back, if there's anyone's client list you should steal it should be his."

"Steal?"

"I don't need your help and I didn't ask for it," she continued. "This whole thing was a big mistake and I suspect that it's just a matter of time before my uncle realizes that, too. And until that time, I'd appreciate it if you just stay the hell away from me. Are we clear?"

"Sofia—"

"It's Ms. Wellesley, thank you."

He blinked unbelievingly. "Are you for real?"

She simply lifted one of her perfectly arched and groomed eyebrows to telegraph that she was dead serious.

"All right." He stepped back. "In that case, no. It's not clear," he said in the same dead tone that she used. "As president of A.F.I., this merger makes *me* second in command of our new business together. Jacob being number one, of course."

Her eyes narrowed.

"So just in case you're having a hard time connecting the dots that means that *you* work for *me*. And I'm no longer asking you to produce your client list. I'm telling you. If I don't have the list in my office before five o'clock today then I'll simply have your assistant compile the list and *I'll* chose which ones you keep and which ones will be divvied up to the other agents."

Sofia's eyes bulged in shock. "You can't do that!"

"Watch me." He turned toward the conference table, snatched up his briefcase and then headed toward the door.

"Five o'clock, Sofia. I wouldn't advise you being one minute late."

He could feel her eyes blazing a hole in the back of his head as he exited the conference room, but at this moment, he really didn't give a damn.

Chapter 3

"**J**ust who in the hell does he think he is?" Sofia fumed as she stormed back down the hallway to her office, feeling as if smoke was coiling out of her ears. Ramell had the nerve to insinuate that *she* worked for *him?* Had the world gone crazy? What was up was now down and vice versa? "Give him my client list? It'll be a cold day in hell!"

An intern looked up and then rushed to move and jerk his mail cart out of Sofia's path before they were both bowled over. The practically comical scene caught everyone's attention, except Sofia's. She was too busy challenging the strength of her Christian Louboutin heels as she continued to pound them against the agency's marbled floor. Never in her professional life had she allowed *anyone* to strong-arm her, and she wasn't about to let Ramell Jordan be the first.

Her boss. Ha! That would be the damn day. The more she thought about his smug attitude back there in the conference room the more she wished that she had said something that would've put him in his place. Anything to wipe that satisfied look off of his face. Sure, he might be decent looking or even handsome by industry standards. Six foot one, close-cropped hair, sexy goatee and fit enough to bounce a quarter off any portion of his body—but none of that meant she was going to allow his well-honed charm to work on her.

No sir.

So what if most industry insiders liked him and she had a few unsuccessful tries at poaching a few of his clients. It just proved that he was good at fooling people. And she didn't even want to get started in thinking about the harem of women he'd collected over the years, never settling down with one for longer than a few weeks. That's a major red flag.

Never mind that she hadn't been able to maintain any serious relationship herself. Circumstances are different for women. Men usually run off screaming from professional women. It had been her experience in Hollywood that men tended to like their women young and dumb, or at the very least women who put in the effort to pretend to be dumb around them. She didn't play that game.

Sofia reached her uncle's office and breezed inside without saying a word to his assistant, Elisa, who was just a little too slow to stop her.

"Um, Ms. Wellesley," she called out feebly as Sofia marched right past her.

"We need to talk," Sofia declared, interrupting Jacob in the middle of his practice golf swing.

Her uncle let out a long breath. "Meeting over so soon?" Jacob glanced at his watch. "I figured that it would be at least another five minutes before Ramell pissed you off."

"I'm sorry, Mr. Wellesley," Elisa said from the door.

"It's all right." He waved her off. "Just shut the door behind you."

"Yes, sir." Elisa rushed to do just that.

"What? Was she supposed to play goalie and block me from coming in here?"

Jacob sat aside his golf club as he admitted, "She was at least supposed to give me a heads-up."

"Very funny." Sofia folded her arms. "Just like I find it *hilarious* that Ramell Jordan seems to be under the illusion that he's my boss."

"Oh good Lord." Jacob headed over to his desk and removed the bottle of Tums he kept in the bottom drawer.

"Want to tell me what that crap is all about?"

"Well, I guess *technically* he is sort of…kind of, your boss. Technically speaking."

"Come again?" she asked, cupping her ear. Sofia wanted to make sure that she heard her uncle correctly before she snapped, crackled and popped off all up in his office.

"Sofia, just listen. Now, I know that you're upset."

"Try pissed. In fact, I think I've just discovered a whole new level of pissed off. I've been busting my butt for years now trying to make full partner, or even take over the family business, and now you go and throw a monkey wrench like this at me. That man out there now has more pull and say in my own father's company than I do! How could you?" She stomped her foot, feeling a tantrum coming on, which was completely unlike her. Sofia prided herself for always being calm, cool and collected, but today's surprises were making that impossible.

"Calm down, Sofia. When I retire, I fully intend to turn the presidency over to you. Ramell knows that and he knows that he will remain vice president."

"But until then…"

"Until then…well, yeah, I guess *technically*—"

"There you go with that technically stuff again." She tossed up her hands. "This isn't going to work. It's just not going to work," she said as hysteria started creeping into her voice. She had worked too hard to cut Ramell Jordan out of her life only for her uncle to undermine all of her efforts now.

"Sofia, what's the big deal? Ramell is a fine business-man with a lot of good and creative ideas to help take this company to the next level. We've known his family for years. They're good people."

"Ha!" She rolled her eyes.

"What is that supposed to mean?"

"Emmett and Ramell Jordan are not to be trusted. I know that for a fact. They have always had their eye out for this company and now you've just handed it over to them on a silver platter without so much as a fight."

"Yes. Emmett Jordan has always expressed an interest

in merging our two companies together. And there has always been an interest on our end to do so."

"Not by my father."

"I think I'm a little more qualified to know what my brother wanted and what he didn't want," Jacob charged back. "I did, after all, start this company with him. I'm also the one who kept the business afloat long before putting you on the payroll."

"Why do I keep getting the distinct impression that you're trying to force me out of the company?"

"Because you're too stressed out and it's making you paranoid." He marched over, turned her around by her shoulders and directed her back toward the door. "This discussion is over. Just trust me on this one. Now get back to work, and try not to stress yourself out too much."

"But—"

"No buts. Just do me a favor and *try* to get along with Ramell."

"I don't know if—"

"That's all. Thanks," he said, pushing her out the door and then closing it behind her.

"How rude." Sofia huffed and stormed off toward her office.

Sarah glanced up from her desk and caught the look on Sofia's face. Instantly she was on her feet, anticipating a list of duties to be rattled off to her.

"In my office," Sofia barked, breezing past her assistant so fast that a small gust of wind ruffled the stacks of papers on Sarah's desk.

"Yes, ma'am. Right away." Sarah grabbed her iPad and rushed in right behind her boss. When they entered the office Sofia seemed content to just pace in a circle. It wasn't just a regular *oh, I'm trying to think* kind of pace. No. Sofia Wellesley looked more like a dangerous wild animal plotting her next attack.

"Is everything all right?" Sarah asked, backing up. If Sofia was going to pounce she didn't want to get too close.

Suddenly, uncharacteristically, Sofia stopped pacing and began to smile. "Sarah!"

"Yes, ma'am?" Sarah asked, taking another cautionary step backward.

With her smile still abnormally wide, Sofia walked over to her assistant and linked her arm through hers. "How do you feel about taking a vacation?"

"Excuse me?"

"You heard me. I want you to leave. Take the rest of the month off."

"A month?" Frowning, her assistant's brows started to stitch together.

"Yes, a month." Sofia insisted as she brightened. "You deserve it. How long have you been working for me?"

Sarah shrugged and stammered, "Um—five years."

"Five years," Sofia repeated. "And you get what—two weeks vacation a year?"

"Well, actually I haven't actually had a vacation in three years."

"Three years?"

"We both haven't," she reminded Sofia.

"Humph." She frowned at that for a moment. "Well there's no time like the present, don't you think?" Sofia started out, directing Sarah back to her desk. "Now you grab your things and I'll just see you next month."

"What? You mean leave right now?" Sarah double-checked.

"Absolutely."

Sarah stopped and dug her heels in. "Okay," she said tentatively. "Am I being fired? Did I do something wrong?"

"No," Sofia reassured her. "It just occurred to me that I've been working you too hard. Your family lives in New York, right?"

"Y-yes. But—"

"Then it's a perfect time for you to go drop in for a visit." Back out at Sarah's desk, Sofia helped the girl by grabbing her purse and leather laptop bags. "Oh, and I need to change your computer pass code." Sofia rushed around to her assistant's computer and started keying in numbers.

Sarah's eyes glossed over. "Are you sure I'm not being fired? Whatever I did wrong, I can fix it."

"You're not being fired. You have my word on that." Sofia popped back up and started escorting her toward the door. "Go. Have a good time. I want you nice and refreshed when you come back."

"Um. Okay," Sarah said. What else could she say? But Sofia didn't just walk her to the door, she walked her all the way to her Honda Hybrid and even stood in the parking lot and waved goodbye.

When Sofia returned to her office, she couldn't help but dance around her office like she'd just scored the final touchdown in a Super Bowl game. Hips shaking and arms waving, she couldn't wait to see the look on Ram's face when she told him that Sarah wouldn't be available to compile him her prized client list and she'd changed the pass code to ensure that no one else could generate the list, either.

"I feel bad that I don't have any cash on me so I can make it rain up in here."

Sofia jumped and spun around to see her new *boss* leaning against her door frame. "What are you doing in here?"

"Well I was enjoying the show. I think you missed your calling. You should've been a dancer."

"And you should have been a jerk. Oops! I forgot. You are a jerk." She rolled her eyes and marched to her desk. "Now if you're finished annoying me…I'm busy."

"Busy getting that list together, I hope."

Sofia cocked a smile. "Tell you what. Why don't you hold your breath and just wait for it?"

"All right. Five o'clock." He tapped his watch.

"I'm not sure if that time frame is going to work for me," she said, flashing him a smile. "I'm really very busy, so you're going to have to wait for Sarah to prepare it."

He glanced over his shoulder to Sarah's empty desk.

"But don't bother looking for her. She's on vacation… for a while."

"Aww. Well that was awfully nice of you, seeing how you work her about as hard as you work yourself."

"Thank you, vice president," Sofia said, before adding under her breath, "of the peanut gallery." She motioned for him to leave her office. "Now if you don't mind."

He didn't move. "Well, I hope Sarah has fun wherever she's going. I'm so glad I got her to compile that list before she went."

"What? You did what? When?"

"After our meeting while you were in the office with Jacob."

Sofia's jaw nearly hit her desk.

"You know, I see why she works for you. She's fast and efficient." Ram winked at her. "I'll review it and get back to you." And with that he strolled off, whistling.

Chapter 4

The Latin Grammy Awards were being hosted in Las Vegas. Limelight Entertainment Management represented a number of Afro-Latin musicians that were nominated for everything from Best New Artist to Best Latin Album of the Year. The awards were always held in November—a good six months after the crazy award season in Los Angeles. It doesn't mean that it was any less hectic—and this year it was doubly so for Sofia because she had foolishly sent her assistant on vacation and she was dealing with a temp, Stewart, that seemed permanently hyped-up on caffeine, had dyslexia when it came to writing down numbers, and had a habit of dropping more calls than a crummy cell phone provider.

If there was one silver lining to this dark cloud, it would have to be that she had managed to avoid Ramell

Jordan for the past seven days. How on earth her uncle thought she was going to be able to control her blood pressure with him around, she never knew.

After Stewart screwed up with Armani on which date she needed her awards dress to be delivered and failed to mail out an e-vite to the nominees for Limelight's pre-award private party, Sofia's patience was pretty much ready to snap when the car that was supposed to take her to the airport never showed up.

"What the hell? Did he think I was supposed to hitch a ride?" Sofia yelled, rushing to throw her bags in the back of her sister's car.

"Calm down," Rachel said, laughing. "It's all good. I don't mind dropping you off at the airport."

Ever since her engagement to Ethan Chambers, it seemed like nothing bothered Rachel anymore; not the drama of working on the set of *Paging the Doctor* or the hectic pace of putting a wedding together or even having her love life splattered across the pages of every tabloid across America. Growing up, Rachel wanted nothing to do with the spotlight so of course life dealt her a hand where she'd fallen in love with the hottest star on television. But when push came to shove, love triumphed.

Rachel glowed like a woman in love and Sofia was surprised to feel a prick of envy. That was unlike her too since she truly wanted the world for her baby sister. And if there was anyone who could give her the world, it was Ethan. Her future brother-in-love was a rarity in this city: a genuinely good man who valued family.

"I got to get Sarah back here pronto or I'm going to

pull out every strand of hair on my head dealing with Stewart."

Rachel laughed and started up the car. "Sounds like you've finally met your match with Ramell Jordan."

Sofia's eyes nearly rolled out the back of her head on that. "Puh-lease. That'll be the day."

Rachel glanced over at the passenger seat while Sofia hooked her Bluetooth on her ear and started powering up her iPad. "What's the deal between you and Ramell anyway? You act like the man is our sworn enemy or something."

"There's no deal. Trust me. I just have to put up with him until Uncle Jacob comes to his senses. And I hope to hell it's soon because the two of us in one office isn't going to work." She tapped her ear and immediately transitioned into her professional voice. "Hello, Akil. It's Sofia. How's it going? Are you and Charlene going to make it to the award ceremony this weekend?"

"You know it," Akil Hutton boasted. "My first nomination for that joint I produced with Pit Bull. I'm all over it, baby." Akil and his label Playascape were the hottest players in the game at the moment and Sofia was thrilled that her newest client, and Rachel's best friend, Charlene Quinn's debut CD was going to drop this spring on the label. Then the surprise of all surprises; while Charlene was down at Akil's Miami home studio she won the mega-producer's heart and landed an engagement ring.

"Good. I trust you're bringing Charlene?"

"Of course. Every man needs someone gorgeous on their arms. In my case it's going to be my beautiful fiancée."

Sofia felt another twinge of jealousy, but she covered it by saying, "That's great. I can't wait to see you both there. Make sure you swing by the pre-award ceremony. Maybe we can set it up for Charlene to do a set. Give the people in Las Vegas a little teaser of what's to come."

"Yeah. Yeah. We can make it do what it do," he laughed.

"Good deal. Catch you later. You can reach me on my cell if you need anything." Sofia tapped her ear and rushed to finish her fourth counteroffer to Larry Franklin for Ethan's next contract.

Rachel shook her head. "Does your brain have an Off switch?"

"Not that I'm aware of," she laughed, but then suddenly experienced a wave of vertigo. "Oh, no." She pressed a hand against the side of her head.

"What's the matter?" Rachel asked, glancing back over at her sister.

"Nothing. I'm...I guess I just got a little dizzy there."

"Are you sure you're all right? Do I need to pull over?"

"Don't you dare. I have to make this flight. I'm probably just dizzy because I skipped breakfast. I'll grab something on the plane." Her finger went back to zooming across the tablet on her lap.

Rachel went back to shaking her head. "Did you get your prescription filled?"

Sofia looked over at her.

"Uncle Jacob told me," she said, answering the un-spoken question.

"Figures. I love him dearly, but lately I swear the man is trying to run my life."

Rachel shook her head. "He's just concerned about you. We all are. Your workload—"

"Oh, Rachel, not you, too." Sofia pinched the bridge of her nose.

"Yes, me, too. You're the only sister I have and I'd kind of like to keep you around a little longer…or at least until you fulfill your duty as maid of honor at my wedding later this month."

"Figures." The two sisters laughed. After another twenty minutes of navigating through L.A. traffic, Rachel pulled into the private airstrip in Burbank where Limelight usually shared a chartered private jet with a list of other high-profile industry insiders. Given how her day was going so far, she had no idea why she was surprised to find that her wonderful temporary assistant *didn't* book her on a flight to Las Vegas.

"Please say that you're joking," Sofia moaned. She had already had her bags unloaded from her sister's car and Rachel had already taken off.

The pretty, plus-size woman behind the counter fluttered a sympathetic smile at her. "No. I'm sorry. And we're all booked up. Everyone is trying to get to the awards ceremony for the weekend."

"I know. That's where I need to get to." She let out a sigh and then tried to rein in her mounting frustration. If she got her hands on Stewart, he was a dead man. "There has to be something we can do. The chances of me getting out of LAX today will be close to impossible."

"I don't know, ma'am. Like I said, every flight is completely booked.

"Are you sure? There has to be some room. I can sit in the back with the stewardess. Hell, I can be a stewardess. Anyone want some time off? How hard can it be to serve drinks?"

Still shaking her head, the lone booking agent held firm.

"I don't believe this," Sofia said, jerking away from the counter only to come face to face with a smiling Ramell, dressed casual in a pair of black jeans and a white short sleeved top. Instantly, Sofia's gaze zeroed in on his arm's bulging bronze muscles. What Ram looked like in a suit versus what he looked like dressed down were two totally different animals; this one much more dangerous to her peace of mind.

When her eyes shifted across the wide span of his chest, her hand started twitching at her side. She had a sudden curiosity of what it would feel like to run her fingers across it or even lay her head against it.

Ram cleared his throat and Sofia's gaze jumped up to his mirrored aviator sunglasses. "Is there a problem?" he asked.

"No," Sofia lied.

"Yes," the woman behind the counter contradicted. "Ms. Wellesley is looking for a flight to Las Vegas. Unfortunately, we're all booked up."

"Oh, is that right?" Ram's smile stretched wider. "If you're looking to hitch a ride, you're more than welcome to ride shotgun with me."

She hesitated.

"It's not a private jet. It's just my own personal plane."

"What? You're a pilot?"

He chuckled. "I got my pilot license before my driver's license."

"I think I'll pass," she said and then tapped her ear to place a call. "Stewart, I need a car."

Ram shrugged his big shoulders. "All right. Suit yourself." He turned and started for the hangar.

"You know what, Stewart. Just give me the number. I'll call them. You just call the airline and—scratch that—get me the number and I'll call them, too." She asked for a pen from the frowning woman behind the desk and jotted the numbers down. "Thank you." She tapped her ear and pulled out her phone to start dialing.

"Excuse me," the counter girl said, interrupting her.

"Yes."

"Let me get this straight. You'd rather call and wait for a car to come get you so you can fight traffic over to LAX where you'll wait for a flight that may or may not be available to Las Vegas rather than just get on the plane that's *right there* in the hangar and can have you in Las Vegas in less than an hour?"

Sofia opened her mouth to confirm that was exactly what she preferred to do when the ridiculousness of such a response hit her. She was a busy woman with a million things to do before Sunday night's award show and she was about to throw away a whole day just because she didn't want to be on a plane with Ramell.

"I think I see your point," Sofia acquiesced. She handed the woman back her pen and then rushed out of the hub. "Ramell! Ramell!" Sofia raced as fast as she could in heels. "Did anyone see where Ramell Jordan ran off to?"

A few of the guys in the hangar just looked up and smiled as she darted by. When she finally spotted Ram strolling casually toward a white and red single-engine plane, she sped up, screaming his name. "Ramell, wait!"

"Seems like I've been doing that half my damn life," he mumbled under his breath before he forced on a smile and turned around. "Yes? What can I *not* help you with now?"

Sofia pulled up, out of breath, which once again drew Ram's attention to her heaving breasts. Good thing his eyes were hidden behind his shades or he would've really embarrassed himself.

"About that, um, flight…?"

"Yes? What about it?" He was not going to make this easy for her.

"Well, I was thinking…" She smiled. "Since you're here and I'm here…?"

Ram folded his arms. "Yeah?"

"Well…I guess it would be pretty silly of me to try to book a commercial flight and fight traffic and whatnot."

"That sort of crossed my mind, too. Well, I actually thought it was more like ridiculous…childish…juvenile."

"All right, all right. I get the picture." She frowned. "So can I hop a ride or not?"

It was definitely her attitude that rubbed Ramell the

wrong way so he said, "No," before he turned away and continued toward the plane.

"No?" she echoed and then had to chase back after him again. "What do you mean 'no'? You just offered me a ride back there in the hub."

"That was then. This is now." He reached the door of his beloved plane and pulled it open.

Sofia huffed out a frustrated breath. "What's the difference between now and then?"

Ram tossed in his lone overnight bag and turned to face her. "Back then I sort of felt sorry for you. Now—not so much."

"W-what?" she sputtered.

Taking a deep breath, Ram crossed his arms. "Has anyone ever told you that you really have a nasty attitude?"

She blinked.

"Well, it can't be towards everyone, I suppose. Seems that most people I talk to actually like you. Your clients and studio executives—they all rave about your work and your professionalism. So that must mean this frosty routine is designed just for me. Though I can't imagine why. I've never been anything but nice to you."

Sofia's eyes narrowed. "Is this about to become a sermon?"

Ram pulled in a deep breath, shook his head and turned away from her. "Goodbye, Sofia. Undoubtedly, I'll see you in Vegas." When he started to climb up into the cab of the plane, Sofia panicked and grabbed him by the arm.

"Wait!"

Carefully removing his shades, Ram turned his head and looked down at the slim fingers that were clutching his biceps.

Sofia tried to swallow what felt like a sharp-edged rock in the center of her throat while an intense wattage of electricity singed through her fingertips she could practically see the fine hairs on her arm stand up.

"Do you mind?" he asked.

His warm baritone managed to break whatever weird trance she'd fallen into, but just barely. "All right." She lowered her hand and forced on a smile, but Ram just frowned and stared at her suspiciously. "You're right. I've been a little…"

"Bitchy," he supplied.

"Short," she corrected. "I was going to say *short* around you."

He rolled his eyes and waited for her to finish.

"It's just that…you know a lot of this…merging stuff… I don't like it."

"Actually yes, you made that pretty clear. But it still doesn't excuse…let's compromise and call it rude, shall we? It doesn't excuse you for being *rude*." He glanced at his watch. "Now if you'll excuse me. I have a ton of things to do before the pre-award party *our* company is throwing for our nominated clients." He turned to climb back into the cab.

"Wait!" Sofia grabbed his arm again. "Are you really *not* going to give me a lift?"

Ram continued to pretend that he didn't feel the heat blazing up his arm when he shrugged off her touch.

"Are you really *not* going to apologize for your rude behavior?"

She dropped her hand again and pulled up straight, but the one thing she had trouble doing was getting her mouth to work.

"See you later."

"OK." Her hand flew back to his arm. "I'm…I'm…" She started coughing.

"You have to be kidding me."

"Oh God, I need some water." She clutched her throat as if it needed massaging to get the words out of it.

"You need to stop wasting my time." Irritation had finally crept into his voice. "I'm not going to stand for you talking and treating me like I'm something stuck on the bottom of your shoe. Whether you want to recognize it or not I'm a man that has worked and earned a certain level of respect. If you can't deal with that then I suggest you march your butt out there on the runway and hitch out your thumb and see if you can catch a ride that way."

She blinked and then finally whispered. "I'm sorry."

Ram cupped a hand around his ear. "Come again?"

Sofia sucked in a deep breath, closed her eyes and spoke louder. "I *said* I'm sorry." After a long pause of silence, she peeled open her eyes. Ram looked as if he was still weighing whether to accept her apology or tell her just where she could stick her apology.

"I mean it. I'm sorry," she added.

Ram nodded. "Fine. I'll give you a lift on one condition."

She should have known. "What is it?"

"That you keep your mouth shut. I don't want you to so much as utter a sound," he said with a narrowed gaze that made it clear that he was being serious. "Think that you can handle that?"

"Ye—"

"Ah. Ah. Ah." He waved a finger in front of her face. "When it comes to you, as far as I'm concerned, silence is golden."

Sofia clamped her mouth shut and then angrily nodded her head.

"Good. Then you got yourself a deal."

Chapter 5

Forty minutes. Sofia just needed to keep her mouth shut for forty minutes. How hard could that be? Turns out, it was pretty hard. Given the fact that she had lost her parents in a plane crash, flying was never her favorite thing. But for the most part, she could deal with it because of all the travel that was needed for her job. But climbing into this plane, much smaller than anything she'd ever flown in, was another thing all together.

"How long did you say that you've been flying?" she asked, clutching her seatbelt.

Ram cut her a look.

"I mean…" She glanced around as they neared the runway. "You're sure of what you're doing, right?"

"It's not too late for you to get out," he said.

Sofia opened her mouth but Ram signaled for her to zip it. *Now look who is being rude.* She sulked down in her chair. But when the plane raced down the runway, she slammed her eyes closed and prayed. Five minutes later, she finally felt safe enough to pry her eyes open. By then they were coasting smoothly through the clouds. "Well...okay. This isn't so bad." She exhaled and tried to relax. "I can do this."

Ram just sighed.

"What? Are you going to threaten to kick me out now?"

"Don't tempt me."

Sofia pulled in a long breath while she stared at his strong profile. She tried to hold on to the years of anger that she'd felt for the Jordans. In her head, she could still hear her father yelling and accusing Emmett Jordan of being a backstabber. From that day on, she grouped father and son together. *But was that really fair?*

She jerked at the rogue question and then squirmed in her seat because she didn't really want her subconscious to answer it.

Ram snuck another glance to his right and noticed how stiff Sofia looked in her seat. "Unbelievable," he mumbled under his breath.

"What?"

"Nothing," he lied with a shrug.

"That was not nothing," Sofia challenged. "What is it? Spit it out."

After a couple of more shrugs, he decided to come clean. "I was just noting how...uptight you are." He looked over at her again and shook his head. "You've changed so much."

She raised her chin indignantly. "I have not."

"Puh-lease. I'm willing to bet that this is the longest you've gone without talking on the phone."

"No it's not."

"I'm not counting when you're asleep, though I'm willing to bet that you don't do that for very long, either."

"That's not true." Even as she challenged his assessment, Sofia reached for her cell phone to check her Caller ID.

Ram laughed. "Look at you."

"What?"

"If you don't know then I'm not going to tell you."

Suddenly self aware, Sofia shoved her phone back into her purse. "Whatever."

"All I know is that the Sofia that I grew up with knew how to have fun," he said with a note of sadness. "She used to let her hair down. Run. Laugh. Play in a field of wild daisies...and even sneak kisses beneath the big oak tree in her backyard."

Sofia's heart skipped a beat. The picture of that long lost girl sprung vividly into her mind and there was a twinge of longing that came swiftly and overwhelmed her. She pulled her face away and stared out at what seemed like an endless sky of white clouds.

"It's like we're floating in a dream," she whispered.

Ram smiled. "That's why I like flying. When you're up here, the world and all its problems just fade away."

Sofia sucked in a deep breath and listened to just the steady hum of the plane's engine and single propeller. It did sort of have a calming effect and there was no denying the beauty surrounding her. "I see what you mean."

He chanced another look at her and was pleased to see the tension in her face had disappeared and her posture had relaxed. Sofia turned her head, met Ram's gaze and fluttered a smile before she remembered that she was supposed to be keeping her distance. Jerking her head away, she then looked at the time.

Twenty minutes.

"I should have known that that wasn't going to last long," Ram commented.

"What?"

"You keeping your guard down." He let a wave of silence drift over them. "Do you really hate me that much?"

Sofia's mouth sprang open, but then her words got caught up in her throat.

"I see." Ram trained his eyes back onto the sky in front of him and pretended that he didn't feel the slight pinch in his throat.

"I don't hate you," Sofia whispered and cleared her throat. "It's just…" She struggled for the right words and then just ended with, "I don't hate you."

"That's good to hear." He shrugged his big shoulders. "Even though I don't quite believe it."

Sofia squirmed in her chair.

"I guess it doesn't matter," he said, but then thought about it. "But it would be nice if we could somehow figure out a way to have some kind of cordial relationship since we are going to be working together."

She sucked in a deep breath.

"And yes, it's still duly noted that you're against the merger. But that's already behind us. Moving forward I think the best thing we can do for our employees is to show a united front. I know that's what your uncle and I both want."

Silence.

"Or not," he amended, feeling his frustrations returning. "It's up to you. We can pit the Limelight employees against the A.F.I. employees and see how far that gets us. But I'm willing to bet not far."

Sofia took another deep breath and then said, "I'm being stubborn, aren't I?"

"That's…one word I would've used." He smiled. "If I was going to keep it PG."

That won a second smile from her. Still she was conflicted about letting go of a grudge she'd held for so long against the Jordans. "How about we strike a deal?"

Ram laughed. "It's always about the deal with you, isn't it?"

"What can I say? Negotiating is in my blood."

He nodded. "All right. What kind of deal are we talking about?"

"My client list," she said, crossing her arms. "No dividing it up. My people are my people."

Ram threw his head back and laughed. "Now why didn't I see that coming?"

"I don't know. Maybe you had mistaken me for someone who gives up."

"Never that, baby girl. Never that." He shook his head. "Well?"

He tugged in a breath. "The point in me taking the list was to lighten your workload."

"Do you want to end the stalemate or don't you?"

His eyes narrowed. "I do, but—"

"Good. You want something and I want something. Let's negotiate."

Boxed into a corner, Ram considered his options. The fact that this is the longest conversation they've had without her storming off or tossing in a few choice words his way forced him to recognize the sweet carrot she was offering. "Your list for peace?"

"That's pretty much it in a nutshell."

"But there's still the issue of you working too many long hours," he said, hedging. "I admit that you're one hell of an agent and a great asset to the company, but let's face it. You can't sustain this workload. You need help and you're too stubborn to admit it or acknowledge it."

Sofia's jaw clenched. "Fine. I'll cut back on my hours."

"To forty hours a week."

"What? Don't be ridiculous. I can do…seventy."

"Lower."

"Sixty-five."

"Lower."

"Sixty?"

"Lower."

"Oh. I give up. You're totally being unreasonable." She shifted in her seat in an attempt to give him her back.

Ram was too busy laughing.

"What's so funny now?"

"You are," he said. "I recall us almost having the same exact conversation when you were telling me that you wanted to date a gazillion boys."

"What?" And then the memory hit her. "Oh." Her face warmed as she blushed. "You remember that?"

His smile returned. "Well I had asked you to marry me for like the millionth time."

"You were persistent. I'll give you that."

"All the good that did me," he mumbled under his breath. "I believe that was the last day we were technically friends." He paused. "In retrospect I think a simple 'no' would've sufficed."

Sofia started squirming again.

Ram felt he was finally getting to her. "What happened?"

The angry voice rising from her father's den played in her head, but she forced it out and lied. "Nothing."

"Yeah. Okay. I believe that." He clicked and rotated a few buttons. "Buckle your seat belt. I'm taking us down for a landing."

Sofia closed her eyes and for the first time felt really ashamed of her behavior. It had to be jarring for a young Ramell to have his best friend suddenly stop talking to him. And the way she'd treated him since. She almost groaned out loud. She had been so wrapped up in her own feelings and angst that she didn't allow herself to see things through his perspective. Stealing another glance in his direction, she made a decision. "All right. Fifty hours," she said. "And that's my final offer."

Ramell cocked a smile. "Sounds like we got ourselves a deal."

* * *

When they landed, Ramell offered Sofia a ride to Mandalay Bay, where the 11th Annual Latin Grammy Awards would be held. It was also where Limelight Entertainment would be hosting their pre-award party and where Stewart had booked her room.

And if Stewart was involved in anything that meant that things were screwed up.

"What do you mean we're sharing a room?" Sofia asked the young gentleman with the Justin Bieber haircut behind the counter. "There must be some kind of mistake."

David, according to his name tag, checked his screen again and then shook his head. "You are with Limelight Entertainment, correct?"

"Yes. But—"

"Then, no. There's no mistake. We have you and Mr. Jordan booked for the Media suite."

"Sounds great to me," Ramell said, smiling and grabbing the envelope with their plastic keys.

"Whoa. Wait." Sofia grabbed his arm with a troubled frown. "We can't share a room."

He stared at her and shrugged. "Why not?"

"Real funny, Slick. I don't think so." She turned back toward the counter. "I need another room."

David blinked and then started typing in the computer, but even as he did so he was shaking his head. "I'm sorry but due to the Latin Grammys this weekend, we're all booked up."

She huffed. "Then I'll just have to go to another hotel."

He shrugged. "You can try, but I'm pretty sure that they're going to tell you the same thing. With press, artists and industry people in town for the ceremony, they'll all tell you the same thing. You might find something out on the old strip."

"Oh God," she moaned. Her cell phone started ringing, but she quickly put it on mute.

"Sofia, it's no big deal. The media suite is a huge room. It's at least…what?" Ram asked David.

"Two thousand square feet," David answered. "There are two bedrooms in it."

"See? It's like an apartment. I'll have one bedroom and you'll have another."

He had a way of making it seem reasonable, but alarm bells were ringing so loud inside her head she could hardly think.

"C'mon," Ram said, turning away. "We both have half a million things to do to get ready for the party tomorrow night."

Sofia remained rooted by the counter as she watched him stroll off toward the elevator bay. *This could not be happening,* she told herself.

Ram stopped, turned and looked at her. "Are you coming?"

Still trying to turn off the bells ringing in her head, Sofia slowly pushed one foot in front of the other while she mumbled under her breath, "I sure hope you know what you're doing."

Chapter 6

It *was* a big suite. Sofia relaxed a little when she walked through door and saw that the media room was in fact like an apartment. A pretty nice apartment, at that. They walked through a long foyer with eclectic artwork on the walls and spare furnishing. That led them to a large living room area with floor-to-ceiling windows. There was a full office area, dining room and then it all split off to a media room that was fully enclosed with a state-of-the-art surround-sound theatre.

"Feel safe yet?" Ram asked, cocking a smile and shaking his head.

"It wasn't that I didn't feel safe," she defended. "It was just that…"

"You don't trust me," he supplied, still smiling.

She opened her mouth to lie, but her phone started ringing.

"Saved by the bell." Ramell said before grabbing his bags and heading off toward one of the bedrooms on the other side of the apartment.

Sofia watched him go. Her eyes drifting down his broad shoulders, narrow waist and then finally his firm butt that damn near hypnotized her. Geez, did this man live in a gym?

"Aren't you going to answer that?" Ram asked without a backward glance.

"Oh!" She blinked out her trance and answered the phone. "Hello."

"Ah, Ms. Wellesley. Thank goodness. We're having a problem with the caterer for tomorrow's party," Stewart said, sounding like he was on the verge of a heart attack. "Plus the party planner hasn't arrived yet and the hotel is insisting that we can't have flamethrowers in this place."

"What? I never asked for any flamethrowers." She smacked her hand against her head and wondered what the hell she did to get cursed with this assistant. "You know what? Don't touch anything. Don't call anyone. I'll be down in a minute." She hurried off to put her bags in the other bedroom, but when she came back Ram was standing in the media room in just a pair of shorts, socks and sneakers. She nearly tripped out of her designer pumps at the sight of his bare and muscular chest, his chiseled abs and powerful legs.

Ramell Jordan had definitely grown up.

Ram slipped a DVD into the media console and turned to see Sofia rooted behind him. He waved a hand in front of her after a few seconds. "Hello?"

Sofia blinked and then shook her head, but even then she wasn't sure that she had successfully broken her trance because he was still standing there before her half dressed.

"I was naked."

His eyebrows rose in amusement.

"I mean—" She coughed and cleared her throat. "I was just about to go downstairs. We're having a few issues with the chest." Cough. "I mean party."

He smiled. "You need some help? I was just going to do this workout DVD, but if you need…"

"No. No. Don't worry. I'm on it. I can handle it."

He frowned. "I'll go get dressed."

"No! Really I got it. I'm sure it won't take but a few minutes." He strolled back toward his bedroom with Sofia's gaze following him again. Once he was out of sight, the spell had finally been broken and Sofia could un-root herself from the center of the suite.

"What the hell?" She pressed a hand against her chest only to discover that her heart was beating like a drum. "I have to get out of here."

Not waiting for Ram, she rushed out of the suite and down to one of the conference rooms Limelight Entertainment had rented out for their pre-award show. She ushered her useless assistant aside and delved into fixing all the problems he'd created.

In between talking with the caterer and apologizing to the very lovely flamethrower that her services wouldn't be needed, Sofia took call after call from clients and studio executives. When suddenly the energy in the room shifted and the hairs on the back of her neck stood straight up, Sofia tossed a glance over her shoulder to see that Ramell had entered the room. She felt a twinge of disappointment because he actually had the nerve to put on more clothes. How ridiculous was that?

She continued to watch him while he moved through the room, talked to a few people and even shared a laugh or two. Despite the conversation streaming through her Bluetooth and her nodding to the caterer, Sofia found herself mentally undressing Ram. She remembered vividly what those muscles beneath that T-shirt looked like, just like she was sure that she could probably grate a block of cheese across his abdomen. Suddenly, she was unbearably hot.

"Is the air conditioner working in here?" She fanned herself.

"Excuse me?" her client asked through her Bluetooth.

"Sorry, Larry. I wasn't talking to you." She glanced around and then reluctantly waved Stewart over.

He rushed over like an overeager puppy. With his big, brown, bewildered eyes, he actually sort of looked like a puppy, too. "Yes, ma'am? You need something?"

Sofia hit the mute button on her call. "Check with someone about the air conditioner. It's hot in here."

He frowned. "Really? I was just thinking it's a bit chilly."

She huffed and rolled her eyes. "Will you please just go do what I ask?"

"Yes, ma'am. I'll get right on it." He actually saluted her and ran off.

She turned back toward the caterer only to see that she

had moved over to Ramell along with the party planner, seeking to get his final approval on Sofia's changes.

What the hell?

She took her call off mute and said, "Larry, I hate to do this to you again, but I'm going to have to call you back."

"Does that mean we have a deal?"

"I'll call you back," she insisted and then walked over to Ramell. "Did I miss something?" she asked, interrupting Caryn midsentence. Both sets of eyes zoomed over to her. "I put the party together every year."

Ramell smiled. "And I'm sure that you've always done a wonderful job. But this year I'm here to help." He signed something for Caryn and then asked. "Do you mind giving us a few minutes alone?"

Caryn nodded and then flashed a smile at Sofia before tiptoeing off.

"What gives?" she challenged.

"Nothing." He shrugged. "I'm just giving you a hand since two doesn't seem like it's quite enough."

Sofia's spine stiffened. "What does that mean? Are you saying that I dropped the ball or something?"

Realizing that he'd put his foot into his mouth, Ram tried to backtrack. "No. No. We've already been over this, remember?"

"Yeah." She stretched the tense muscles in her neck. "We've also been over the fact that I didn't ask for your help."

Ram's smile melted off his face. "That's because you're stubborn." When her face darkened he knew that she was just seconds from exploding. "Can't you just relax? Or don't you know how to do that anymore?"

"I—" Her phone rang. She reached for it only for Ram to snatch it out of her hand. "What are you doing?"

"They can leave a message. We're talking. You and me," he informed her.

She blinked and started sputtering.

"I need you to understand something. I gave you back your client list, but my objective is still to lighten your workload. You can go along with it or we can upend that truce we've had for the last—" he glanced at his watch "—two hours and go back to our respective boxing corners."

She sucked in a breath and lifted her chin. "I just don't like being pushed around."

"And I don't like pushing you," he said in a softer tone. "I really don't, but I feel like you're forcing my hand on this."

She scoffed.

"Unbelievable." He shook his head. "I knew that you were a workaholic but this is ridiculous. What do I need to do? You want me to hog-tie you and stuff you in your room upstairs to make you take a break? Is that it?"

"What?"

"Because I'll do it." He tossed up his hands. "Hell, why not?"

She stepped back from him. "You wouldn't dare!"

He leveled a stern look at her that made it impossible for her to discern whether he was joking or not. Hit with another wave of vertigo, Sofia wobbled around on her heels.

Ram quickly reached out and steadied her. "Are you all right?"

"Yeah," Sofia lied and then tried to push her way out of his arms, but the steel grip he encased her in refused to budge.

"Someone bring us some water," Ram snapped to no one in particular.

Everyone scrambled. The next thing Sofia knew she had her pick of at least fifteen water bottles. "Uh, thanks," she murmured, accepting one.

"Drink," he ordered.

For once, she did what he said. The moment the cold water slid down her throat she sighed out loud, but it was questionable whether it did anything to cool her down or cure her vertigo. In fact, she started to suspect being locked in Ram's arms and feeling the hard ridges of his chest up close and personal were only making things worse.

"How do you feel?"

Ram's intense gaze bore into hers to the point that she was having a difficult time getting her breathing under control. "Fine," she lied again, and attempted to push away again.

Ram loosened his grip, but he didn't let her go. "That settles it. I'll take care of the party. You go upstairs and lie down."

"Ramell—"

"That wasn't a request. I'm telling you." The look he gave her dared her to argue back. "I got this. Get upstairs. Take a nap. I'll be up there in a little while and I'll check on you."

"I'm not a child."

"Then stop behaving like one," he snapped back.

She wanted to argue back, but what was the point? Ramell was proving that he was willing to lock horns and go toe to toe with her. But feeling that they were the center of attention, Sofia knew that it was time to back down. "All right. Fine. I'll go take a nap or something."

"No 'or something'. A nap." He finally released her, but she remained pressed against him for a few extra seconds as if her body wasn't really ready to leave.

With a weak smile she stepped back. "I guess I'll just catch up with you later." She reached to retrieve her phone, but Ramell held it back.

"No. I think I'll just hold on to this."

"What?"

"The last time I checked, you don't need a phone in order to take a nap."

She crossed her arms. "It's not like there isn't a phone in the suite."

"Maybe not, but without an address book, I'm thinking that you'll be limited on who you can call."

She opened her mouth to argue again, but stopped when she watched him huff and start to roll his eyes. "Fine."

"Good. I'll check on you later." He tossed her a wink and then strolled off.

Frowning, Sofia watched him go, her mind undressing him once again. "Snap out of it," she hissed, and then rushed out of the conference room. Once she was away from Ramell her head started to clear.

"Ms. Wellesley," Stewart shouted and raced down the

hallway toward her. "I talked to the hotel management and they said that they will send someone to check on the air conditioner." A big, eager smile bloomed across his face. "Is there anything else I can do for you?"

"I, um...actually, just go ahead and take the afternoon off. Mr. Jordan will be taking over the preparations this evening so that actually gives us some time off."

Stewart's bushy eyebrows jumped up. "*You're* going to take some time off?" he asked, practically laughing.

"What?"

"Look. I know I haven't been on the job long, but I was told that you didn't believe in taking time off."

She frowned, feeling insulted. "Who told you that?"

He shrugged as if it was no big deal. "Everyone at Limelight...and everyone at the temp agency...and I think I might have read it in the trade papers, too."

"Come on, I'm not that bad." Sofia laughed, but Stewart just gave her a timid smile. "Am I?"

"I don't think that I've been around long enough to say," Stewart answered tactfully.

"Well played. I get the point." She marched off with her feelings still bruised. "Everyone acts like I don't know how to relax," she mumbled. "I know how to relax." Her gaze darted around the beautiful hotel. It was filled with people laughing and smiling—just generally having a good time.

"I know how to have a good time." She shimmied her shoulders a bit to try and relax them, but then started to feel silly. At the elevator bay, she hit the Up button and waited. A second later, a laughing couple waltzed up next to her to wait, as well. But Sofia started to feel uncomfortable when they started kissing. She turned her back toward them and shook her head. She never really cared for people who got carried away with public display of affection.

The elevator bell dinged and Sofia hopped into the compartment and pushed for the twentieth floor several times. The couple was so into trying to swallow each other's tongues that she breathed a sigh of relief when the doors started to close.

"Wait! Hold the door!" someone shouted.

The couples' lips un-suctioned and the guy jammed a hand between the doors before they could close all the way.

Damn.

"Thanks," Ramell said, appearing out of nowhere and springing into the elevator.

"Not a problem, man." Mr. Don Juan cheesed and then escorted his girl inside the compartment, as well.

Ram's eyes drifted over to Sofia. "Good. You're actually on your way up to the room."

"Why you coming to check on me so soon?" Sofia asked as the elevator doors closed.

"Now why would I do that?" He mustered on a faux innocent look and blinked his eyes at her.

Sofia didn't have a chance to answer because Mr. Don Juan suddenly hiked up his lady's leg with one hand and hit the floor panel with his other hand. Eight floors worth of lights lit up. "Oh my God," she moaned in sync with the woman that was busy getting felt up.

Ram glanced over at the couple and chuckled.

"It's not funny," Sofia hissed, annoyed.

"Oooh." The woman moaned as her lover now concentrated on grabbing her ass and unbuttoning her blouse with his mouth.

"You're right. It's not funny." Ramell whispered.

"Thank you," Sofia said, satisfied.

"It's actually kind of hot," he said.

"What?"

Just then the woman's bra spilled out of her top and the man's mouth lowered so that he could run his tongue along the lacy edges.

Sofia gasped while Ram cocked his head to try and get a better look. "Will you behave?" She shoved him by the shoulder.

"What?" Ram laughed.

The elevator doors opened on the third floor and Sofia ran out like the damn thing was on fire. "I can't believe this!"

Ram followed her. "What's with you?"

"Hey, you two don't want to watch?" Mr. Don Juan asked as the doors started to close again.

Ram looked at Sofia as if the answer depended on her.

"No!"

"Suit yourself," the man said, and then returned to trying to peel his girl out of her clothes.

After the doors closed, Ram turned and looked at her. "Well, that would have been interesting."

"You're joking. Please say that you're joking." She hit the button for another elevator.

He shrugged his shoulders. "It's Vegas," he said.

"People do things that they don't normally do. You know that."

She shook her head. "Men!"

"What? What did I do?" Ram couldn't stop chuckling. "Those two could be married for all we know."

"No rings."

"You did a ring check?"

"That's better than what you were checking out. A couple of more seconds and you would've been nipple bobbing, too."

"Now I'm offended," he said, placing a hand against his chest.

"Sure you are."

"I am. Anyone who knows me knows that I'm more of a leg man." He deliberately let his gaze drop to her long legs. "And if you ask me, you have the best pair I've ever seen."

Sofia blushed, but was spared from having to make a comment when another elevator arrived.

Ram followed her. "So you're really upset about that?"

"It was…inappropriate."

"And I take it that you've never done anything inappropriate?"

"Well…not like that." She frowned, not even able to imagine herself ever losing so much control that she would behave like a twenty-dollar trick. "I have a little more self respect than that."

"Then like what?" Ram asked.

"What do you mean?"

"Tell me about a time when you've done something inappropriate."

Sofia drew in a deep breath and did a quick search of her memory banks.

"Nothing?"

"Wait a minute. Let me think," she said. They arrived on their floor and she waltzed out the elevator. She was still thinking when she slid her key into their suite and hadn't come up with anything.

"How about something spontaneous?" Ram chuckled. When that only deepened her frown, he decided to let her off the hook. "Never mind. I don't want your brain to start short-circuiting."

"So maybe I haven't done anything that's technically inappropriate or spontaneous. Big deal. It doesn't mean that I'm a prude or anything."

"All right. If you say so."

"It doesn't," she insisted.

He shrugged his shoulders and started to walk off.

Suddenly hit with a burst of inspiration, Sofia grabbed Ram by his hand and pulled him back. When he turned laughing, she cupped both sides of his face and laid a kiss on him that was so powerful he couldn't help but let out a grunt of pleasure. He raked one hand through her thick hair and settled the other against the small of her back. Ram couldn't believe how sweet she tasted or how soft her small curves were. Was this a dream?

Sofia pulled her lips back all too soon but he chased after them for another intoxicating dose. It only lasted for a few extra seconds before she pushed back.

"There," she whispered, while gulping in air. "Is that spontaneous enough for you?"

Before he could answer, she stepped past him on wobbly knees and quickly rushed toward her room before she spontaneously ripped his clothes off.

Behind her, Ram watched her go with a widening smile. Things were finally moving in the right direction.

Chapter 7

Sofia couldn't sleep, not for a nap or even later on that night. All she could think about was that damn kiss. It had to have been some trick of her mind to make her think that the man tasted like chocolate and honey. And even while she lay tossing in her bed, she kept running her tongue across her mouth for any residue he might have left. That kiss disturbed her peace of mind and she wondered if she could ever view him the same way again.

It also seemed like the more she told herself not to think about it, her brain just kept looping the memory of her cupping his face and then moving in on those incredible soft lips. Those few little stolen kisses they used to share under the big oak tree at her parents' old estate was nothing to compare to what Ramell delivered in the living room of that suite. If she kept it up, she was going to drive herself crazy.

She had kissed him to prove that she could be spontaneous and step out of her comfort zone. Now she feared that she'd just opened Pandora's Box. Even knowing that, she wanted to kiss him again. There was a part of her that wanted to prove that what she felt was a fluke—a trick of the mind. Another part of her wanted to kiss him because she hoped like hell it hadn't been a fluke but something greater, something more.

The second the sun rose the next morning, Sofia showered, dressed, and zoomed out the suite so fast it was amazing she hadn't left skid marks. All she knew was that she needed to get as far away from Ramell as she possibly could. Her first pit stop of the morning was to get breakfast inside the hotel's restaurant, Verandah. The minute she entered the Mediterranean-style restaurant and the smiling hostess led her to an available table out on the terrace, her racing heartbeat settled a bit.

"Sofia!"

She glanced around and then spotted Charlene Quinn waving a few tables over. "Hey!" She popped out of her chair and went over to say hi to her newest client. When she reached her, Sofia leaned over and gave the glowing singer a hug. "How are you, sweetheart?"

"Great. How are you? I tried to call you when we arrived but my calls kept going to voicemail."

Sofia lightly tapped her hand against her head. Ramell still had her cell phone. "I'm so sorry about that. Did you need anything?"

"Aww. Look who we have here," Akil Hutton approached the table. "How you doing, baby girl?"

Sofia laughed as she now exchanged hugs with the super producer. "You know me. I'm still out here swimming with the sharks."

"I hear that," he said, taking his seat and then leaning over to plant a kiss on Charlene's glossy lips.

They look good together. "I know I said it before, but I want you two to know that I'm really happy for the both of you"

"Thanks," Charlene cooed, her right hand entwined with Akil's.

They were so adorable together that Sofia couldn't stop smiling at them. "So. Are you all set to perform this afternoon at our pre-awards gala?"

Akil bobbed his head. "Yeah, we set everything up with your man, Ramell."

Sofia laughed, but it sounded a little off note even to her ears. "Ramell Jordan is *not* my man." She tried laughing again but it was still sounding like a misfired weapon.

Akil frowned. "Nah, I meant it as a figure of speech. He's your business partner, right?"

"Oh, yeah. Right." *Open mouth, insert foot.* "I knew that. My man."

Akil shared a look with Charlene and then smiled back up at Sofia. "Anyway, like I was saying, we set everything up with Ramell. We're going to do a sound check around two and then we'll be ready to go on at five."

"Sounds good." Sofia gave them both a thumbs-up. "I guess I'll just see you at the party."

They said their goodbyes and Sofia rushed back over to her table and ordered herself a stack of buttermilk pancakes. Given the fact that she generally burned the candle at both ends most days, her lifestyle afforded her the luxury of being able to eat whatever she liked. So she ordered a large stack of buttermilk pancakes and link sausages. She was practically salivating when they arrived at her table. After thanking the waitress, she figured she had about fifteen minutes before she needed to meet up with Stewart and get her day going.

When the list of things that she needed to get done before the pre-awards gala started scrolling through her mind, Sofia crammed food into her mouth as fast as she possibly could.

"Mind if I join you?"

Sofia glanced up with a sausage poking out of her mouth.

Ramell smiled. "You know, you could've woken me up. Breakfast is the most important meal of the day."

Cheeks crammed with pancakes, Sofia gave him a half apology but then felt a wave of panic when he took a seat.

"Now that's an interesting look," he chuckled. "The chipmunk cheeks look good on you."

The waitress returned and sat his breakfast of French toast and scrambled eggs down in front of him.

"So how did you sleep last night?"

Sofia's eyes narrowed. She had a sneaky suspicion that he knew damn well that she hadn't slept a wink. When he continued to wait for an answer, she lied. "I slept like a log." She smiled animatedly.

His eyes twinkled. "Glad to hear it."

You're playing with fire. Sofia tried to swallow her food but suddenly realized that she needed help.

"Here. Have some of my orange juice." He pushed his glass toward her.

"Thanks," she murmured around the breakfast that was clogging her throat. She quickly gulped down half the glass and then panted when she finally managed to clear her pipes.

"Better?" His neatly groomed brow stretched over his forehead.

She nodded and dabbed the corners of her mouth with her napkin.

"Are you in some kind of hurry or do you usually eat like a starved animal?"

"Ha. Ha. Very funny."

"Well it was either those two options or…you're trying to avoid me so that we don't have to talk about that kiss we shared yesterday."

Sofia shoveled in another hardy helping of pancake into her mouth so that she wouldn't have to respond.

Ram laughed so hard his head nearly rocked off his shoulders. A few curious gazes drifted toward their table and Sofia suddenly wished that she could shrink down to about two inches.

"Do I really make you *that* nervous?"

"Don't be ridiculous," she barked and then started to choke.

Tears practically brimmed his eyes as he watched her weak performance.

"Actually, I don't have much time to eat. There's a lot I have to do before the party and the award show."

He sobered up a bit. "Anything I can help you with?"

"No. I have everything under control. Or maybe I should ask whether you need any help with the party. I know things can—"

"Nope. Everything is fine and going according to schedule."

She frowned. "Nothing ever goes according to schedule."

"They do if I'm handling it," he said confidently.

"Right." She tossed down the rest of his juice and then scrambled up from the table. "I'll catch up with you later."

"Looking forward to it."

For the next few hours Sofia remained busy, with Stewart getting some of her clients to press junkets, and answering emails on her iPad. Most of her workload was difficult without her phone, but she lacked the courage to ask Ramell for it back. She didn't have a stack of pancakes on hand to help her through another round of questions about that kiss.

Of course that kiss never stopped looping in her mind, either. It happened so much, in fact, that people were constantly snapping their fingers in front of her face and asking if she was all right. A little after noon, Stewart reminded her that her hair and make-up artist was scheduled to meet with her in the suite so she rushed up to go get ready for the afternoon festivities. Everything was running smooth until the Armani representative, Robyn, showed up.

"That's not the dressed I ordered," Sofia said frowning. "I requested the white ball gown with the big butterfly bow in the back."

The petite rep blinked in surprise and then quickly scrambled for her paperwork. "I have here that you asked for the gold drape halter."

Sofia sucked in a breath. She could literally feel her blood pressure rising. "Where are my pills?" She rushed off toward the bathroom and downed one of the much-hated pills.

"Are you all right?" Robyn asked nervously when Sofia returned to the room.

"I will be," she said, pulling in a few measured breaths.

"I'm not sure what to tell you" the rep said. "I spoke to Stewart myself and—"

"Stewart? All he was supposed to do was arrange the delivery date—not select my dress. *I* had selected my dress." *Breathe. Breathe.* "You know what? Never mind. What do we have to do to fix this? How fast can we get the other dress here?"

Robyn blinked and then glanced at her watch. "I'm sorry, but I'm afraid that just can't possibly happen. Your gala is in less than an hour."

Breathe. Breathe. That was hard since at that moment all she wanted to do was find Stewart, wrap her hands around his thick neck and squeeze.

"Don't you want to just try it on?" Robyn asked.

"It doesn't look like I have a choice now." Stripping out of the hotel's robe, she quickly stepped into the gold dress and glanced into the full-length mirror while Robyn zipped her up. Her anger immediately dissipated.

"I think it looks beautiful on you," Robyn complimented.

Sofia turned and assessed herself from different angles. She actually liked it better than the dress that she had picked out originally. "Looks like Stewart actually got one right." She shook her head. "Amazing." The dress was short, hitting her around mid-thigh, and the shimmering gold color reflected beautifully off her mocha skin. And it felt fun and flirty when she did practice turns.

After filling out the paperwork for the dress, Sofia rushed to put on her accessories while the woman took her leave. When Sofia exited from her bedroom, Ramell was in the living room sliding into his tuxedo jacket. They stopped and stared at one another. At that moment, Sofia was convinced that Ramell Jordan looked good in everything.

"Wow. Don't you look amazing," he said.

She blushed—that was something she had been doing a lot of lately. "Thank you. You don't look so bad yourself." Approaching him with slow, measured steps, Sofia noticed that Ram's tie was slightly off-center. "Here. Let me help you with that."

Ram smiled when her slim fingers quickly went to work with his tie. Being this close he was able to get a good whiff of her perfume. On her first go around, she actually made the tie worse off than it was before so she had to try again. While she concentrated on the tie, he kept drinking in her beautiful profile while fighting the urge not to kiss her again. The more he kept trying not to, the more he wanted to do it.

After a minute, he started to give into gravity and lean forward. She would probably stop him, slap him or give into the kinetic energy he knew that she had to feel flowing between them. When he was within an inch of her lips, her fingers stopped fiddling with his tie.

"What are you doing?" she whispered.

"Something spontaneous." His lips gently landed against hers and stirred up old feelings deep within him. She moaned first and then he pulled her closer. Thrilled and surprised that she was allowing herself to go with the moment, Ram experienced a renewal of hope of what was possible between them.

Their lips only pulled apart because of the necessity of oxygen. And even then he pressed his forehead against hers so that their breaths could commingle.

"What are we doing?" she asked, panting.

"Something that we should've done a long time ago." He reached up and brushed the side of her face.

"But I…I—"

"Shh." He kissed the tip of her nose. "Don't worry. I'm not trying to rush you or anything. Understand?"

She slowly nodded.

"Take your time. I'm not going anywhere." His hand moved from her subtle cheek down to beneath her chin where he tilted her face upward gently. "But know this, I do want you. I always have…and I always will."

He watched her large brown eyes widen and she pulled back just a bit, but didn't run off screeching toward the bedroom. At least that was a good sign. He gave her a wink and then offered her his arm. "Shall we go?"

Sofia hesitated for a second, drew a deep breath and then finally looped her arm through his. "I guess I'm as ready as I'll ever be."

He cocked his head, hoping her answer held a double meaning. When they arrived downstairs for Limelight's Official Pre-Award Gala, they were both thrilled to see that everything had come together perfectly. The event's color scheme was black and gold; it was a nice blend of fun and sophistication. Only after arriving did Sofia realize that they were the same colors that she and Ramell were wearing.

As their guests entered the room, Stewart and a few interns working with the party planner directed people over to the table where hundreds of goodie bags were lined up.

Over the speakers played the music of all the Latin Grammy nominations for the evening. The infectious rhythms instantly had Sofia rocking her hips in time to the beat.

Ram turned toward her and started dancing with her. "Looks like you have some good moves. Should we take this to the dance floor?"

She laughed. "I don't think so. This is as good as these moves get right here. A dancer I am not."

His gaze raked over her. "I beg to differ."

Sofia couldn't quite get used to this constant flirting

that they were now engaged in. "Well, maybe I'll just give you a rain check."

"All right. But I will cash that sucker in before the end of the night." He winked. A tray of champagne floated by and Ram quickly chased it down and then offered her a flute. "Let's make a toast."

"That sounds like a good idea." She accepted the glass. "What shall we drink to?"

"To us," he said, simply.

Her brows rose.

"…and our new business merger. May we enjoy years of success together."

She relaxed a bit and then tapped her glass to his. "To us."

Their eyes locked over the rim of their flutes while they each downed a sip of champagne. Just a few short moments later, they separated as they networked through the crowd. At exactly five o'clock, Akil Hutton took to the small stage and introduced his newest artist to the Playascape label.

The guests applauded as Charlene Quinn made her way over to the microphone. Feeling slightly giddy, Sofia couldn't wait until Charlene opened her mouth and shocked everyone with her powerful voice. When she did there was a collected gasp. Charlene wasn't the barely legal teenybopper that could only carry a note with the help of Auto-Tune, which was all the rage in music nowadays. Charlene was a beautiful and welcome throwback artist who could do things with her voice that could only inspire envy. Listening to the emotional song

"The Journey," Sofia's gaze drifted across the room and had no problems finding Ram in the crowd.

Luckily there was another tray of champagne drifting by so she quickly snatched up a glass and drank its contents just as Charlene was hitting the song's climatic ending. The room erupted into thunderous applause. Charlene smiled humbly and thanked everyone before stepping off the stage.

The second glass of champagne must have gone straight to Sofia's head because suddenly she was feeling…good. She looked across the room again and locked eyes with Ramell.

Damn good, in fact.

Chapter 8

The Eleventh Annual Latin Grammy Awards was a unanimous hit. The evening was filled with spectacular music and dance. All of the performers were magnificent and the cheers from the crowd just made the evening feel like a four-hour-long concert. Akil Hutton won his first Latin Grammy and gave an emotional shout out to the new woman in his life, Charlene Quinn, and then of course reminded everyone to look for her debut CD coming out in the spring.

After the show ended, everyone started drifting out of the venue to head for some of the many sponsored after parties. Sofia and Ramell made their way over to the Eye Candy Sound Lounge. Sofia loved its high-tech touch tables that allowed people to project images over the dance floor. Ram wrapped an arm around her waist and shouted over the music.

"I think I'll take that dance now!"

"You got it." Sofia quickly tossed back her chocolate martini and then slipped her hand into his. With the multicolor-lighted disco floor and the strange electronic images floating overhead, Sofia was experiencing a sensory overload—and she loved it. She threw her hands up in the air and rocked her body to the beat like she didn't have a care in the world.

Never being more than a few inches away, Ram matched each erotic thrust of her hips with one of his own. In no time at all it was just them and the music. Sofia was saying things with her body that she never dared to say aloud. If he touched her hip, she'd touch his. A few times, she'd turned around to roll her butt up the front of his crotch, swivel her hips and then spin away.

Ram was so turned on that he couldn't think straight. He had never seen this side of Sofia before. She was sexy, wild and making him horny as hell. After about an hour on the dance floor, they returned to their table and ordered a few more drinks.

Sofia ordered another chocolate martini and when Santana's "Smooth" blasted through the speakers, she climbed on top of the table along with a few other girls and shook her moneymaker for all it was worth.

Ram bobbed his head along with the music and mouthed the chorus when his eyes met with Sofia's. *Give me your heart, make it real. Or else forget about it.* The seductive smile she shared gave him such a strong hard-on, it was a wonder that he didn't just sweep her off the table, toss her over his shoulder and take her back to their suite. But he made sure that she could read that thought in his mind.

Eventually, she did hop down and Ram was right there to catch and spin her around. There was a skip in his memory because the next thing he knew they were actually at a roulette table, a game Sofia claimed she had never played before, but was suddenly begging to play. Thrilled to see her smiling and having a good time, Ram removed a few Benjamins from his money clip and handed them over.

The croupier exchanged the money for chips with the pit boss watching and then asked everyone to place their bets. Sofia took all of her chips and placed them on five.

"Are you sure?" Ram asked.

"No. But that's why they call it gambling," she reminded him, and then planted a loud, smacking kiss on his lips.

"Then let's let it ride."

"No more bets," the croupier called and then proceeded to spin the wheel.

Sofia locked her arms around Ram's neck and proceeded to watch intently as the white ball was dropped into the spinning roulette. "Are you having a good time, Mr. Jordan?"

"Actually, I'm having a wonderful time," he answered, sliding his hands up and down her back.

"Five! The lucky number is five!" the croupier called out.

Just as Sofia was about to plant a kiss onto Ram's lips, she realized the number that had just been called.

"Five! That's me! That's me!" She started bouncing up and down. The entire table erupted into cheers while Sofia performed a mini-dance and then smacked Ram hard on the rear end.

Caught off guard, he jumped and then laughed at her antics. They played for a few more rounds, the crowd cheering as Sofia's chips really started to mount. More drinks flowed and the next thing Ram knew they were at the craps table. Sofia developed her own dance and threw the dices down the stretch. Each time she would draw a seven and their entourage would grow even larger.

"You're hot tonight," Ram commented, shaking his head.

"Yeah? So what are you going to do about that, lover boy?" She playfully pulled on his tie so that she could draw his lips closer. When she laid another kiss on him, the table went wild with hoots and hollers.

"God, I have to bring you to Vegas more often," Ram panted when she finally released him.

Sofia just smiled. "Let's go find another dance floor."

"Your wish is my command." He handed over his V.I.P. card and informed the pit boss to cash them out and that they'd pick up their winnings later before leading her and their entourage out of the casino and over to another after party at Pure nightclub.

As the hour ticked later and later, both Ram and Sofia's dancing grew hotter and hotter. They drew many eyes and much finger pointing, but neither paid any attention to it. They were both ying and yang, grinding on the dance floor and just enjoying the night. Sofia couldn't remember the last time she had ever felt so free, so alive. Every time Ram's gaze roamed over her body she felt beautiful and sexy. If she had her wish, this night would never end.

Somewhere along the line, someone in their newfound entourage suggested going to a club called Jump! So they all piled into a stranger's limousine and ended up at another high-tech club. The surprise was that it was a strip club, but not just any strip club.

"Oh hell no." Ramell said and turned right back around toward the door.

"Wait. Wait." Sofia grabbed him by the arm and dragged him back. "C'mon. This could be fun."

Ramell groaned as he allowed her to turn him back around. His frown deepened at the sight of the muscled and oiled men all pumped up and gyrating on the stage. "I don't want to watch this."

Sofia ignored his complaints and pulled him along. He wasn't the only one. A lot of the guys that had played tagalong were also trying to make their way back toward the door. However, the women were going buck wild, including Sofia, who continued to drag Ramell closer toward the stage.

He hung his head and hoped that this was just going to be a pit stop. When the dancer finally left the stage with his teeny-weeny briefs filled with dollar bills, he expelled a sigh of relief.

"You should go up there," Sofia yelled above the crowd.

"Say what?" He tried to pull back.

"C'mon." She smiled. "You can do it." She kept pulling him toward the stage despite his horror.

When the women saw what she was doing they all started cheering.

"What's this now?" The D.J. blasted over the club. "Is it amateur night on the stage?"

The women screamed louder while Sofia shoved Ramell harder.

"C'mon. You know you got the body," she teased.

"I'm not getting up on that stage."

The D.J. spoke out again over the loudspeaker. "Let me give you a little something to dance to, my man." He began to spin a popular new song and the women in the club damn near went into hysteria.

"Fine. If I have to get up here then so do you," Ramell said as he grabbed Sophia by the wrist and pulled her onto the stage alongside him.

Suddenly, the lights dimmed and a spotlight was directly aimed at the couple. Sofia stood in the center of the stage, giggling until she felt a feathery touch drifting down her arm. She shivered but then she was quickly spun around to see Ram rip the buttons off his shirt with one-hard jerk and then do a sexy body wave that had the women screaming so loud it made her eardrums ring.

Ram sent his shirt sailing into the air and rocked his hips as he pulled up his white t-shirt to reveal his perfectly bronze chest with his tight, mountainous muscles.

Without thinking, Sofia reached out and smiled at his dewy texture. Smiling, Ram spun her around and pressed her back against his chest while his large hands dropped to her thighs and then slowly inched their way upward. The heat that blazed up Sofia's body was so intense that beads of sweat dotted her hairline and rolled down the side of her face.

The women that were screaming around the stage no longer mattered. Sofia was losing her mind because she alone could feel Ram's hard-on grinding against her round bottom. It was suddenly hard for her to breathe. His hands inched higher and when he was just a flick away from exposing her Victoria's Secrets, he whipped away from her again to perform a few more body waves and hip rotations.

Money rained down onto the stage despite the fact that Ram never took his eyes off of Sofia. He crooked his finger and beckoned her toward him. When she stood inches from him, he unsnapped the top button of his slacks and offered her, and her alone, a peek inside. Curiosity may have killed the cat, but Sofia wasn't about to pass up a golden opportunity. So she peeked and her jaw nearly hit the floor at his impressive size.

The women went wild. They all wanted to see what she saw. But with her face heating up, she finally slapped a hand in front of his pants and prevented him from peeling those bad boys off. Suddenly, she wasn't in the mood for sharing. "Don't you dare."

"Problem?" he asked, wickedly.

She grabbed hold of his wrist and tugged him off the stage.

"Boo!" The jilted women shouted, but a giggling Sofia and Ram paid them no mind as they tried to make

their way to the door. They were still laughing when they piled into a cab and headed back to Mandalay Bay.

"You know I look ridiculous, right?"

She glanced at him without his shirt and T-shirt and decided, "Actually, I think I prefer you like this."

"Really?" He dragged her over to his side of the cab and pressed her against his chest.

"We can always arrange it so that I could see you like this more often," she said, walking her fingers up his chest.

Ram's brows jumped. "I'm listening."

Smiling up at him with her hand pressed over his heart she asked, "Ramell Jordan, will you marry me?"

Chapter 9

At three-thirty in the morning, Sofia and Ramell stumbled into the Viva Las Vegas Wedding Chapel, giggling and clinging on to one another. Behind them, Akil and Charlene entered, shaking their heads. They were still dressed in their gown and tuxedo, only Akil had draped his jacket around Charlene's exposed shoulders as they came in from the night. It was clear that they didn't know what to make of this latest development. They were surprised when Ram called them as they were leaving yet another after party. Both of them looked exhausted and might've been headed for bed had Ram not called and asked if they wanted to serve as witnesses to his wedding.

"Are you two sure that you want to do this?" Akil asked.

Charlene nodded. "Yeah. This seems kind of sudden. Maybe you guys should just…sleep on this?"

Sofia laughed and wrapped her arms around Ram's waist. "Don't be silly. Ram and I have been planning to get married for…" She looked up at him. "How long?"

He smiled. "A gazillion years."

They erupted into giggles while Charlene and Akil just looked at each other and shrugged.

A black Elvis Presley impersonator emerged from a curtain of multi-colored beads with a grin as wide as Texas. "Evening, folks. What can I do for you on this early morning?"

Sofia and Ramell took one look at the man in his bedazzled jumpsuit and had another fit of giggles. This time, even Akil and Charlene joined in.

"Are we looking to have a double wedding this morning?" he asked eagerly.

"No. It's just us," Sofia answered excitedly.

"First, do you happen to have a shirt I can buy or rent?" Ram asked.

"Sure. We can hook you right up," Elvis bragged and then disappeared into the back.

While he was gone, Sofia and Ramell peppered each other's faces with kisses. To casual observers they looked like young lovers who couldn't keep their hands off of each other. When Elvis returned he held up two suits. One was a pale blue suit complete with bell bottoms and satin lapels. To add insult to injury, the accompanying white shirt had enough ruffles to do Liberace proud. The other suit was a black and silver sequin number that was equally hard on the eyes.

"Just a basic white shirt will do," Ram said, snickering. "I may be drunk but I'm not *that* drunk."

Elvis shrugged his shoulders. "As you wish." He disappeared and returned with a brand new white dress shirt still in its package.

"Perfect."

"Great." Elvis clapped his hands together. "Now let's see about getting you two married."

For the next ten minutes Elvis showed the couples rings and different wedding packages. They settled on the Elvis Blue Hawaii Special, mainly because it came complete with two traditionally garbed hula dancers. Sofia and Ram giggled their way through the entire ceremony. Still they managed to get their I Do's out and were immediately showered with rice while Elvis busted out with his microphone and launched into a jacked-up rendition of Blue Hawaii. He didn't really bother trying to sound like the King of Rock-n-Roll. If anything he sounded more like Isaac Hayes. But it didn't matter. Nothing really mattered at that moment.

They were married.

Amazingly, after they left the chapel they all stopped at another club so they could share a celebratory drink. There was more dancing involved and Sofia stopped nearly everyone she saw to show off the simple silver band and declare that she was indeed a married woman now.

Cheers went up and cameras came out. Sofia and Ram made several silly poses. At long last when the hour ticked closer to five o'clock, Sofia struggled to keep her eyes open.

Ram stretched up a brow. "I don't believe it. My little Energizer Bunny is actually wearing down?"

"Mmm-hmm." Sofia looped her arms around Ram's neck and nibbled on his lips. "I think it's time we get back to our honeymoon suite."

"Aww. Honeymoon suite, eh? I kind of like the sound of that." He kissed her and explored her mouth like it was the eighth wonder of the world. She moaned and melted against his body.

"Get a room," a member of their second entourage shouted, causing everyone to laugh around them. In dramatic form, Ramell swept Sofia up into his arms and received a round of applause.

Sofia smiled against his lips. "I'm so happy right now."

He met her gaze. "That's all I ever wanted you to be."

"Good to know." She snuggled closer. "But if you want to see me ecstatic then I suggest you get me to our room, lover boy."

"I'm on it." He turned toward the group. "Good night, everyone. Me and the missus have plans."

"Woo hoo!" they all cheered.

"Say goodnight, Sofia."

"Goodnight, Sofia," she chimed, giggling.

With that, Ram swooped out of the club and carried her all the way over to the hotel portion of the luxurious casino. In the elevator, Sofia insisted that she wanted to be the one to punch the number for their floor, only for her to do it with her left big toe. "Hey! What happened to my shoe?" Not until that moment did she even realize that she was just wearing one.

Ram frowned. "I have no idea."

"Oooh," she pouted. "But I loved that shoe."

"Don't worry," he said, nibbling on her lower earlobe. "I'll find it for you."

"You promise?"

"Yeah. I promise. Now kiss me."

"Gladly." She turned her head and captured his addictive lips in another soul-stirring kiss. Sofia loved kissing this man. She loved how her thoughts would get all woozy and how her body would heat up and tingle from the tips of her toes all the way to the ends of her hair.

Neither one of them heard the elevator again or even saw another couple step into the small compartment along with them. They were in their own world where only they existed. Ram lowered her legs, but kept her body pressed up against him and one wall of the elevator.

Sofia couldn't stop moaning as she felt her husband's hands roaming up her long legs and traveling up her inner thigh. When his seeking fingers skimmed along the edges of her lacy panties, she quivered. But when he shifted them over to the corner of her thigh and then dipped his fingers into the dewy lips to tease the tip of her sex, she nearly came unglued.

"You like that, baby?" he asked, abandoning her kiss-swollen lips in order to concentrate on her sexy scented neck.

"Uhm, hmm." Sofia's eyes fluttered open and she was finally able to see that the same couple they had shared an elevator ride with yesterday was now gawking at them. In normal circumstances she would have been embarrassed, but right now all she could do was giggle.

Ram lifted his head. "Oh. So this is funny to you now?"

She shook her head and then pointed over her shoulder.

He turned and then offered the couple a smile and a wink. "Morning," he said, lowering his hand from beneath Sofia's dress. A bell dinged and the door slid open to offer their escape route. "Have a good day." He took Sofia's hand and together they raced out of the elevator.

Sofia clamped her other hand over her mouth and started laughing so hard her sides hurt. It didn't help that she was hobbling with one shoe on and one shoe off. "Did you see their faces?"

"Forget about them." He waved it off and slid his card key into the lock and then surprised her by sweeping her back into his arms.

"I believe that this is tradition," he said, and then picked her up to carry her over the threshold.

"Weeee!" She waved her hands high over her head as Ram then proceeded to spin her around. Suddenly everything was funny so they just looked at each other and cracked up. Soon enough their laughter faded and their smiling eyes shifted into desire.

"Well, Mrs. Jordan, what would you like to do now?"

Those wonderful tingles returned. "I don't know. I

was sort of hoping that we can do what most newlyweds do on their wedding nights."

He stretched one eyebrow high up on his face. "See. That's the reason we're so perfect for each other. We think alike." He kissed her again. "My bedroom or yours?"

"You choose." She started pulling on his shirt, popping off one button at a time.

"Let's start off in your bedroom. Maybe we'll go to mine on round two."

"And for round three?"

"Damn. We might have to stop for a bowl of Wheaties and a vitamin B shot."

"You do what you have to do, baby." She drew his lips in for another kiss while he walked her toward her bedroom. Unfortunately, since he was distracted by her hungry kisses, he whacked her head against the wall as he moved down the hallway.

"Oww."

"Oh. I'm so sorry." He chuckled. "Are you okay?"

Laughing herself, she rubbed the top of her head only to have him do it again when he made a turn into her bedroom and she hit the door frame.

Thump!

"Ouch. Are you trying to kill me?" she laughed.

"When you're with me, I want you to see stars, baby," he joked, and then finally set her down.

"One way or another." She laughed. Like before, their laughter slowly faded and the chemistry that had always existed between them started to crackle. Suddenly she felt small standing in front of him. But not vulnerable.

The idea of being devoured by a man of his size and strength actually triggered an anxiousness that had her entire body vibrating. One part of her wanted to say *don't hurt me* while the other wanted to shout, *take me however you want me.*

"Turn around," he ordered.

With a smile, Sofia did.

Gently, he swept her long hair over her left shoulder in order to expose the back of her neck. Lightly, he planted small kisses along her shoulders while he slowly unzipped her dress. When he peeled the thin straps from her shoulders, her breathing thinned and she became lightheaded once again.

"Do you know how long I've waited for this night?" He moved toward her collarbone. "How long I've dreamed about making love to you?"

She shook her head though the question intrigued her.

"A gazillion years," he said, spinning her around as her dress fell to the floor. Before she could respond, he crushed their lips together. In his head it was as if the heavens had opened their golden gates. He made quick work of unhooking her strapless bra. When it fell to the floor and her full breasts stood at attention before his greedy eyes, he knew without a doubt that he could die a happy man tonight.

"You're so beautiful." He cupped her breasts with his large hands and then smiled when he felt her tremble. "So beautiful," he repeated, rubbing the pads of his fingers against her nipples. In no time at all they were as hard as marbles and she was panting like she was in the middle of a marathon.

"Do you mind if I taste you?"

"Please," she begged.

Ram's head dipped low and then he sucked one hard nipple into his mouth, lightly scraping the sensitive flesh against his teeth. She hissed and then quivered, letting him know that he had set off a mini-orgasm. He did it again and received the same results. Her trembling hands cupped his head, her fingers raked through his close-cropped hair. He eased her down onto the bed, their hands and mouths exploring one another.

Sofia no longer cared that she could hardly breathe. She just knew that she needed Ram inside her as fast as possible. However, he wasn't on that same game plan. His slow and deliberate moves made it clear that he was in no hurry. He wanted to taste and savor her for as long as possible. Her heart raced like a thoroughbred in the Kentucky Derby. It all seemed like so much but not enough at the same time.

While Ram feasted on her breasts, she lowered her hands from his head and glided them down his neck and then across the wide span of his back. But that was as far as she could go since he started to inch down her body, his mouth planting wet kisses directly down her center. The pleasure was so intense that tears started to leak from the corners of her eyes.

Ram discovered her G-spots were her right nipple, her belly button, and the tiny area on the back of her left knee. To him she looked like a lost angel, quivering and thrashing among the bed's pillows. He took one leg and slipped off her lone metallic shoe before peppering kisses around her ankle and then working his way upward. Her moans grew louder when he reached her thighs. By the time his lips brushed against the crotch of her panties, she was calling on God. But what he longed to hear was his name falling from her lips.

His hand roamed to her slender hips and then peeled her delicate panties off. With the morning sun now peeking through the windows, he liked the way the golden rays highlighted the V of brown curls between her legs. It was like her own private halo.

"So beautiful," he whispered again while parting her legs. Her glistening pink bud peeked through her brown lips. Ram sucked in a breath as he reached down and spread her open for a better look.

With a groan, he dropped his head and lapped his tongue gently against her feminine pearl. Instantly her knees rose up while she sank deeper into the bed.

"Oh, Ram," she sighed.

His heart took flight at the sound of his name falling from her lips. Ram's light laps became a quick and steady drumming. The sweetest honey he'd ever tasted dripped and then poured out of her body until it completely coated his tongue. And still it was not enough.

He settled further down the bed until his abs laid flat against the mattress and her legs were hooked over his shoulders. He looked like he was just settling in for a good meal.

However, Sofia's long legs wouldn't stay still. They kept fluttering on the side of his head like a big butterfly. Then an unmistakable pressure started to build in her lower belly and her manicured toes started to curl. Her eyes sprang wide open as if suddenly realizing that it was all too much. No way could she handle what was coming.

"Ram. Ram, baby." She started inching up the bed.

He knew what was happening, but he showed no remorse. Grabbing hold of her hips, he locked her in place and then transformed his drumming tongue into a whirling tornado.

"Ohh, ohh, yes." Sofia reached out and grabbed hold of the sheets as if somehow they would anchor her down.

"Oh, yes! Oh, yes!"

It went from a tornado to a hurricane in two seconds. The cry that ripped from her throat was undoubtedly heard in the suites surrounding them, but neither one of them cared. After the explosion, Sofia's body continued to tremble with aftershocks.

Ram sapped up the rest of her honey and unlocked her legs that had clamped around his head and then climbed his way back up her body.

"Oh God. I've never felt anything like that before," she panted.

The compliment inflated his ego. "I've just gotten started," he promised.

"No," she said, shaking her head. When he frowned, she added, "I want to do something for you first." She shoved at his shoulder and rolled him over onto his back. Smiling and giggling, she took the top position.

Ram stared up into her beautiful face and still had a hard time believing that any of this was real. Twenty-fours hours ago, he'd just barely gotten her to agree to a truce and now she was his wife and in a few minutes she would completely belong to him.

"You're not the only one who knows a few tricks," she told him.

"Is that right?" He couldn't help but grin.

"Uh-huh." She leaned down and started raining small kisses across his chest. "Oh God. You smell incredible," she moaned.

"I'm glad that you approve." He chuckled.

Sofia's mouth roamed lower. "Mmm-hmm. You taste good, too."

Slowly, she sank lower.

Ram started evening out his breathing in anticipation of his new wife's next move. But then the kisses grew lighter and softer and then he couldn't feel them at all. He waited a moment and then opened his eyes. "Sofia?"

Silence.

He pushed himself up onto his elbows and looked down. Sofia's head laid across his stomach, her arms relaxed against his side and her breathing slow and steady. Is she asleep?

"Sofia?" He reached down and shook her.

"Mmm," Sofia moaned and poked her lips like she was giving him an air kiss. In the next second, she snored. Loudly.

Ram dropped his head back down against the pillows and started laughing. "I guess my little Energizer Bunny has finally conked out."

Covering his face with his hands, Ramell went ahead and had a good laugh. When that was over, he carefully sat back up and awkwardly maneuvered himself up from under his wife. After that, he climbed out of bed and picked her up so he could tuck her in. But before he could join her, he took a very cold shower in her bathroom. It was a sad substitute. When he got out and wrapped a towel around his body, he could already tell that he was cruising toward one hell of a hangover. But damn he had fun.

Just as he was about to exit the bathroom, his gaze drifted over to a medicine bottle. He picked it up and recognized the name of the blood pressure medicine because his father used the same brand name. *Did Sofia take this before drinking last night?* He glanced back out into the bedroom, wondering.

Chapter 10

Riiiinnng! Riiinnng!

Sofia groaned and tried to bury her head deep beneath the pillows. Somehow that only caused the ringing to grow louder. It didn't help that her head felt like it had been crushed beneath an avalanche of rocks. She groaned louder and shot her hand out to the nightstand and consequently knocked a whole lot of things onto the floor. A cacophony of noise caused her to flinch and smack her hands onto the pillows in another lame attempt to drown out all sound. But that didn't stop the ringing.

Riiiinnng! Riiinnng!

This was it. She was going to die. That had to be what was happening to her. Something shifted next to her. She didn't even care what it was as long as it could stop that damn ringing before her ears started to bleed. Something started to climb over her. It was large and heavy and managed to press her deeper into the bed. Great. Now she had the choice of either the noise killing her or being crushed to death. Whichever it was she prayed that it would be quick.

"Hello?"

Sofia frowned at the growling baritone. It was foreign and familiar at the same time. But it didn't concern her enough to try and lift her head from beneath the pillow.

"What do you mean who is this?" the baritone asked. "Who are you?"

Couldn't this floating voice keep it down? Couldn't he see that she was too busy trying to die peacefully over here?

"Oh hey, Rachel."

Rachel? Didn't she know a Rachel?

"You must be looking for your sister," he groaned. "Hold on."

The weight was lifted off of Sofia and she pulled a little more oxygen into her lungs. Before she could seize the opportunity to drift back off to sleep, something started shaking her. Were they in the middle of an earthquake?

"Telephone," the baritone said.

Sofia groaned, wanting to tell the floating voice to keep quiet. Surely any minute the ceiling was about to cave in on them. That would be an interesting way to go. Finally the shaking stopped.

"Sofia, it's your sister," the voice persisted.

Sister? She tried to think for a second and then slowly

she was able to recall something about her having a sister.

"Sofia." The bed started shaking again.

She was seconds away from just starting to cry. "Will you please stop yelling?"

There was a rumbling chuckle. "I'm sorry, baby. But your sister is on the phone."

Baby? Sofia attempted to lift her head, but it plopped back down when it felt as if it weighed a ton. Suddenly, the pillows were magically lifted and the cold phone was pressed to her ear.

"Talk," the voice instructed.

"Hello," she croaked and then cringed at the sound of her own voice. Was she speaking through a megaphone?

"Sofia! What's this about you getting married?" Rachel shouted. "It's all over the trade papers here. Everyone has been calling me all day. Charlene called and told me that she and Akil attended the wedding. What happened? What's going on?"

Rachel hurled questions at her so fast that Sofia questioned whether or not her sister was even speaking English. "I don't… I don't know what you're talking about."

"I'm talking about you getting married! I can't believe it. You beat me and Ethan down the aisle."

Did she just say that Ethan was beating her? Sofia attempted to sit up again. This time succeeding in that she was able to prop her back against the bed's paneled headboard, but there was still no way for her to pry her eyes open. "I'm sorry. Now what did you say Ethan did?"

"What? Ethan didn't do anything. I said that you and Ramell beat me and Ethan down the aisle. I can't believe it! I always suspected that he had a thing for you, but I never dreamed that you two would elope in Vegas."

Sofia's head was pounding so hard that her little sister's sentences weren't making any sense. But her heart quickened at the thought of Ramell eloping. *Her* Ramell? Well, he wasn't technically hers but… "Slow down, Rachel. You're not making any sense. Who did Ram marry?"

Silence.

"Rachel?"

"Are you joking?" her sister asked.

"Joking? You're the one that called me. I'm trying to understand what the hell you're talking about. Oh, God. Someone shoot me, my head is about to split open."

There was another beat of silence before Rachel tried again. "Sofia, are you all right?"

Silence.

"Sofia?"

"Um." Sofia rubbed her head and tried to recall the previous night, but instead she started drifting back off to sleep.

"Sofia!"

"Aah!" She jerked the phone away from her ear and dropped it. "Stop all that yelling," she groaned and then tried to rub the pain away. Next she grabbed the comforter and slid back down into the bed. When she tried to pull the bedding over her head, she got hit in the face with the phone. "Oww." She placed the phone up to her ear. "Hello?"

"Sofia, what the heck is going on?"

"What do you mean what is going on? What are you doing calling this early in the morning anyway?"

"Early? What are you talking about? It's five in the afternoon. I've been calling you all day."

"Five? It can't be that late. I have to be back in L.A. at…" she yawned, "Some time."

"Sofia, focus!" Rachel snapped. "We are talking about you and Ramell getting married."

"Ramell is getting married?" Her heart quickened. "Whoa."

"What?"

"I think I just experienced déjà vu. It seems like we just had this conversation."

"We did just have this conversation," Rachel said. "Ramell *did* get married."

"To who?"

"To you!"

"Me!" Sofia laughed, slapping a hand over her forehead. "Don't be silly! Where would you get that ridiculous idea?"

"But…wasn't that him who just answered the phone?" Rachel asked.

"No…that was…." Sofia drew a blank. "That was…" The floating baritone resurfaced in her mind. *Who was that?* Her head swiveled to the left, over to the huge lump that was buried beneath the covers.

"Sofia?" Rachel inquired.

Sofia didn't answer, mainly because her heart had now found a new home in the center of her throat. With her head still pounding and her hand sweating, she reached out and grabbed the top of the comforter and slowly started to pull it off from whatever or whoever was lying beside her. When the bedding inched away and revealed Ram's peaceful sleeping face, she screamed, dropped the phone and scooted sideways so fast that she toppled out of bed and hit the floor with a thud.

Ram jumped up like a toasted Pop Tart. "What? What's going on? What's happening?" His head swiveled around while his hands went into instant defense mode like he was about to karate chop the first thing he saw.

"What are you doing in my bed?" Sofia barked.

Ram's head jerked to his right, but when he saw the bed empty, he had to lean all the way over to the heap piled on the floor. "What are you doing down there?"

"I asked you first." Not until his gaze began to roam over her did he realize that she was naked. "Close your eyes!"

"What?"

"You heard me. I said close your eyes!" He started laughing at her. *"Now!"*

He tossed up his hand and closed his eyes. "All right. All right. They're closed. Are you happy?"

Sofia reached up and snatched the comforter from off the bed and covered herself. "I'm still waiting for an answer," she snapped. "What the hell are you doing in my bed?" It no longer mattered that her head felt like it had its own personal jackhammer drilling away or that in her fall she jerked the telephone cord out of the wall socket. She needed answers and she needed them now.

"Well?"

"I don't think that I understand the question," he

said, leisurely lying down on his side. "I know that I'm a little hungover right now, but I definitely remember you inviting me into this bed."

"I most certainly did not!"

"You most certainly did. When I carried you into the suite, I asked you 'My bedroom or yours?' and you said, 'You choose.' Then I said 'Let's start off in your bedroom. Maybe we'll go to mine on round two.'"

Sofia gasped. "Liar!"

"What?" He laughed, not taking her charge seriously. "You even suggested that there might be a round three. Which there wasn't, by the way."

Her eyes grew larger with each word he said. "Are you saying that we…me and you…*had sex?*"

Ram's frown deepened as if he didn't know how to take this strange interrogation. "Well, I guess that would depend on your definition of sex."

"What do you mean?"

"Well, we definitely flew past first, second, and maybe even third base. It was sliding into home where we sort of fell apart."

Sofia grabbed her head. She was still having a hard time trying to process any of this. "But why…I don't understand. Why would I…why would we…?"

"Well, it is what most people do after they get married."

"Get married?!" She jumped up onto her feet but forgot the comforter.

Ramell's smile returned when his gaze caressed her small curves. "No worries. We can easily just pick up where we left off," he said, peeling back the sheets so that she could see that he was hard and ready.

Sofia gasped, but her eyes zoomed in on Ram's thick and sizable member. For a moment she experienced a surge of recognition.

He started patting the bed. "Don't worry. I won't bite…unless you want me to."

His body was like a huge magnet and Sofia felt herself pulling toward him. But she quickly slammed her eyes closed and tried to shake off whatever spell or voodoo had come over her. "This is not happening," she recited to herself. "This has to be a dream…or a nightmare… or something."

"Careful," he warned. "I think you're on the verge of hurting my feelings."

Sofia's eyes flew back open and, sure enough, Ram was still lying on the bed in his beautiful birthday suit. "Oh, my God." She dropped down and snatched up the comforter again. But it was one sudden move too many. Her stomach rolled while her gag reflexes were activated. She dragged the comforter up with one hand and then slapped the other hand across her mouth to buy a little more time while she raced toward the bathroom.

"Are you all right?" he asked.

She didn't get far before tripping over the long comforter so she dropped it and continued her race toward the toilet. Once there, she dropped to her knees and proceeded to expel the many drinks she consumed the previous evening. "Oh God," she moaned when she managed a half of a second to breathe. A moment later, she was hit with another wave of soured alcohol.

"Poor, baby." Ram retrieved a face towel from one of the racks and quickly wet it with cool water. Once he ringed it out, he made it over to the toilet and started pressing it against Sofia's hot face and neck.

Sofia glanced over at him and was relieved and a little disappointed that he'd put on a pair of boxer shorts before coming in to help her.

"Shh. It's going to be all right," he assured her while he pulled her long hair out of the way. "Just try to take deep breaths."

She closed her eyes and tried to follow his instructions. When the towel started to warm, he rushed back over to the sink and ran cold water over it again. It took awhile before everything started to settle down and she was able to look up at him. "Are we really married?"

He nodded. "If memory serves me correct."

She didn't know whether to throw up again or start crying. How could something like this happen? Why couldn't she remember… "Wait. Was it by a black Elvis impersonator?"

A smile lit Ram's face. "Aww. You do remember."

Sofia turned back toward the toilet and threw up.

An hour later, Ramell helped bring his hungover wife back from the brink of sickness. He pumped her full of fruit juice and crackers to get her amino acids up. After that he gave her some Excedrin for her headache and then helped her to the shower. Through it all, he had to admit that he liked taking care of her. While she was in the shower, he ordered himself a mini-buffet since they had missed both breakfast and lunch.

He started cleaning up the bedroom while he waited. It was busy work so that he didn't have to think about what Sofia would say once she came out of the shower. Judging by her reaction to the news of their marriage, he had very little hope that they would reach their two-day anniversary.

He plugged the phone back into the wall just as the bathroom door swung open. Ram looked up to see Sofia draped beneath a white hotel robe that was at least two sizes too big. Even with her hair wet and no makeup, she was still the most beautiful woman he'd ever known.

"We need to talk," she said.

"I had a feeling you were going to say that."

The phone rang. He picked it up because it was already in his hands. "Hello."

"Ramell," Jacob Wellesley roared. "What's this I hear about you marrying my niece?"

"Uh, Jacob! Hello!" He glanced over at Sofia.

Her eyes bugged out as she started shaking her head.

"Well?" Jacob demanded.

Ram couldn't tell whether his new business partner was mad or just sincerely wanted an explanation. "Yes, sir. About that, I'm sure it has come as a bit of a shock but—"

"Shock? Hell, I'm wondering what on earth took you so long!"

"Yes, I, um…what did you just say?"

"I said that it took you too damn long," Jacob laughed. "I can't tell you enough how thrilled Lily and I are about this latest development."

"Oh, really?" He looked back over at Sofia who was now mouthing questions to Ramell, trying to figure out what her uncle was saying.

"This just means that I made the right decision in merging our companies together. Plus, it means that our business is still technically family-owned. I have to be frank with you, I've been up nights worried about all of this. Now I feel as if a giant load has been taken off my shoulders."

"It does?" he asked.

"What?" Sofia whispered, creeping over to him.

Jacob continued. "I was up every night. Doing this deal made me feel like I was somehow stabbing Sofia in the back. She has worked very hard in the company and in a lot of ways I should have made her full partner years ago. At the same time, all those hours she puts in had us all worried. Now that you two are going to officially be a team, well…I know that you're going to look after her best interest and not let her take on too much. Frankly, I think you are a Godsend."

Ram smiled. "I can't tell you how much it means to me to hear you say that, Jacob."

"You love her, don't you?" Jacob asked.

Ram's gaze caressed Sofia's face while he spoke from the bottom of his heart. "For as long as I can remember."

"I knew it!" Jacob's laughter thundered through the phone so loud that Ram had to pull it away from his ear for a second. "Is she there right now? Her aunt and I would love to talk to her."

"Yes. She's right here."

Sofia shook her head and backed up.

"He wants to talk to you," Ram insisted.

"No. No." Ram thrust the phone under her ear. "Noooo— Hi, Uncle Jacob." She forced a smile into her voice, but gave Ram an evil look.

"Congratulations, Sofia," Uncle Jacob boasted. "I was just telling your husband how thrilled your aunt and I are about this wonderful news! Even though I question the venue you and Ramell selected. A black Elvis impersonator?"

"What? How did you—?"

"It's all over the news. The media followed Akil Hutton and his new girlfriend there thinking that they were about to get hitched and instead got tons of footage of you and Ramell getting married. It's a little unconventional, I admit, but it looks like it was a lot of fun."

"We were on the news?" Her gaze shot back over to Ram.

"Don't look at me," he hissed. "You're the one that proposed to me."

Sofia covered her hand over the phone. *"What?"*

He shrugged. "I take it you don't remember that part, either."

"Clearly. I was drunk out of my mind," she hissed. "Why didn't you stop me?"

"You seemed fine to me. Besides, I was drinking, too," he reminded her.

"Hold on, Sofia," Uncle Jacob interrupted her next retort. "Your Aunt Lily wants to talk to you."

"Wait, Uncle Jacob."

"Sofia?" Her aunt's soft voice drifted over the line. "Baby, is that you?"

Sighing, Sofia dropped down onto the bed. "Yes, Aunt Lily. It's me."

"Baby, I'm so happy for you," she sniffed. "I've always suspected that you two had strong feelings for each other. And I prayed for so long that someday you both would get together."

Sofia frowned. "You did?"

Her aunt laughed. "Please. I think we all did. I remember back in the day that boy must've proposed to you every day of the week. Your mother and I used to find it adorable."

The mention of her mother instantly brought up many conflicting emotions that glossed her eyes with tears.

"Aww. You used to tease that boy mercilessly," Lily said. "Personally, I'm thrilled that he hung in there. You two are perfect for each other—but for a while it seemed like you were determined not to realize it."

Sofia didn't understand where all this was coming from. People thought that she and Ramell were perfect for each other? Sure, once upon a time she used to fantasize that one day they would get married, but that was a long time ago. She was only a child.

"Aunt Lily, I think that there's something I should tell—"

"The only thing I hate is that we all couldn't be there—Elvis impersonator and all."

"Yeah. About that—"

"So you have to let me throw you two a big reception. It'll be tight since we're still planning Rachel's wedding and all, but you *have* to let me do this. I've been looking forward to this day for so long."

A long pause hung over the phone while Sofia tried to come up with the right words. Instead of admitting that she was just seconds from telling Ram that she wanted an annulment, she said. "We would love for you to throw us a reception, Aunt Lily." Her gaze jumped back up, this time to see Ram's startled face. "Nothing would make us happier."

Chapter 11

While Ramell and Sofia headed to Los Angeles, they were still dancing around just how they were going to handle this whole marriage thing. Their cell phones and emails were overflowing with congratulatory messages from friends, colleagues, studio executives and even tabloid magazines and bloggers. For a moment, they were being treated as if they were celebrities themselves. The embarrassing part was just how much of their wild night was documented.

In the world of camera phones, it seemed that every-where and everything they did that night ended up somewhere on the web. Ramell made it clear that he liked the ones with her dancing on club tables. For Sofia, it was the video of Ramell's debut strip performance.

"I would've gone Full Monty if you would've let me," Ram said while he flew them into the private airport.

"That would have played well on *Entertainment Tonight*," she chuckled.

"I want to know why you stopped me," he said, glancing over at her.

"Maybe because even in my drunken state I realized that we needed to hold on to *some* dignity."

"Or maybe you didn't want to share me with all those other women," Ram suggested. "I kind of like the idea of you being possessive."

"Oh, please." She straightened herself in her seat while her fingers flew across her iPad. She was rapidly transforming back into her old self, with her ever present Bluetooth hooked onto her ear and her ability to type ninety words while still holding a separate conversation.

Ram shook his head. "Do you have to do that now?"

"Do what?"

"Work. We have a lot of stuff to figure out, Mrs. Jordan."

Her fingers tripped over themselves at the sound of her new title. She wanted to be irritated, but the truth of the matter was that her heart quickened a little bit whenever he called her Mrs. Jordan and parts of her even tingled a little. *What the hell is going on?* She glanced over at him and met his smiling eyes. One thing was for sure, Ram certainly didn't seem bothered by landing himself a new wife at all.

She forced her gaze away and coughed. "What sort of stuff do we need to figure out?"

"Oh, I don't know. Things like…where are we going to live?"

"What?"

"You don't think that it might be a little strange that if we return home and go back to living in separate houses?"

"I guess that's a good point," she conceded, and then thought about it for a moment. "How about my place?"

"You live in a high-rise."

"Yeah, so?"

"So. Now that we're a married couple maybe a house is more appropriate?"

"Meaning your house," she said, crossing her arms.

"I do happen to have one available," he reasoned. "And you don't have to worry, I have excellent taste. It's not your run-of-the-mill bachelor pad."

"Says you."

"Says everyone. It was actually featured in *Architectural Digest* last summer. Of course, I had to take down the sex swing, but if you want we can get it out of the attic."

Her head whipped back over to him.

"It was a joke. Ha. Ha. We're supposed to laugh at jokes, remember?" Ram reached over and elbowed her playfully. "You really need to learn how to lighten up."

"Have you ever thought that maybe you play too much?" she challenged. Now she had to try to get the image of her riding on his swing out of her mind, even though she was partly intrigued.

"One can never play too much, sweetheart."

It was the endearments that were doing her in. *Baby,*

sweetheart, honey, Mrs. Jordan. Each one sounded and felt like a lover's caress and was undoing the foundation of everything she thought she knew about herself.

"So would you like to go out with me when we get back home?" Ram asked.

"Excuse me?"

"Well, it sort of just occurred to me that despite our knowing each other for all our lives, we haven't officially gone out on a date."

"We don't have to date." Sofia shook her head. "We're married now."

He laughed. "Yeah. I guess we sort of put the cart before the horse here. But I'd like to take you out. Plus, I hear that married couples are bringing dating back with a vengeance."

She shook her head but a smile curved across her lips.

"Does that mean we have a date?"

Sofia tried to stifle the small flurry of excitement fluttering in the pit of her stomach. Why was she feeling like this and why couldn't she stop it? Self-discipline was something she prided herself on, but since Ram charged back into her life it'd been more or less thrown out of the window entirely.

"Yes? No? Maybe so?" he asked.

"Well where do you plan on taking me?"

"Ah. Ah. Ah." He took his hand off the controls to wave a finger in front of her. "I want it to be a surprise."

She lifted her eyebrows but still couldn't wipe the smile off her face. "All right. Fine. May I at least know when this post-marriage date is going to take place?"

"Sure. How about tomorrow night?"

"Oh. I don't know if I can do tomorrow night." She pulled up her calendar on her iPad. "I think—"

"Whatever it is, cancel it," he said.

"What?"

"You heard me. Cancel it." He gave her a look that made it clear that he was being serious. "I think that with everyone knowing that you're a newlywed they will be more than forgiving of you canceling whatever it is you seem to think is so important."

"My business *is* important."

"You mean *our* business, right?"

She opened her mouth to continue arguing, but once again realized that there would be no point. Ramell had a cool, logical answer for everything. "Fine. I'll cancel."

"Great! See, now that wasn't so hard, was it?"

She folded her arms with a huff and pretended to be annoyed. At least that would have been true a few days ago. Lately, she was finding his take-charge attitude to be a real turn-on. Maybe there was something else in her blood pressure medication because ever since she started taking those things, she hadn't been acting like herself at all.

With just a few minutes left in their flight, Sofia leaned her head back and closed her eyes. But she was totally unprepared for the images that splashed in her mind. Images of Ram sliding off her shoes and of him kissing her on her ankle and then working his way up her inner thigh. Her body started tingling like crazy. She drew in a soft breath, sure her body temperature was rising.

The pictures inside her head were so vivid she swore that she could feel his fingers peeling her panties from off her hips. She squirmed in her chair.

"So beautiful," his voice echoed inside her head as he parted her legs. When his head dropped in between them, Sofia's eyes sprang open.

Ram looked over at her, concern written on his face. "Are you all right?"

Panting, Sofia placed a hand over her heart and stared at him.

That only made his frown deepen. "Sofia?"

"Y-yes. Yes. I'm fine," she lied. *Was that a dream or a memory?*

He gave her a look that said he didn't believe her, but he let it go.

They touched down at the airport and they were both surprised to see a few photographers waiting there, snapping away.

Sofia was thrown off guard. While her agency may represent some of the most talented people in Los Angeles, the spotlight rarely hit her personally nowadays. It was a little reminiscent of the days after her parents' death. She couldn't imagine why anyone would be interested in the life and times of a Hollywood agent in the tabloids, but there they were.

Ram quickly escorted her to his white Porsche and peeled out of there as if he was trying to qualify for a drag race. While he played speed racer, Sofia glanced around the spotless, leather interior.

"What?"

She shrugged. "Nothing. I was just thinking that this is the sort of car a confirmed bachelor would drive."

"Well, just say the word and I'll trade this puppy in for a minivan in a heartbeat."

He grinned devilishly at her and she had the sneaky suspicion that he meant it. *Kids?* Things were definitely moving too fast for her to wrap her brain around. They were going to start dating after getting married and now they were going to discuss kids before they had sex? Or did they have sex already?

Another image of Ram's head dipping low to suck one of her nipples into his mouth filled her head along with him running his teeth lightly against the sensitive tip. She twitched and her panties grew moist. She covered a hand over her mouth when she could hear her own sighs echoed in her ears.

"Are you sure you're okay?" Ram asked.

"Yes," she said as she started fanning herself. "Don't you have an air conditioner in this thing?"

"It's cool and the windows are down," he said.

"Well… I'm hot." She reached over to the console herself and put the air on full blast.

Ram just gave her a stern look and then shook his head. What man really understood women anyway? He was trying to wing this whole marriage thing himself. So far, Sofia hadn't said anything about getting an annulment, but she wasn't exactly acting like a gushing newlywed, either. Hopefully on their first official date tomorrow, he could put all his cards on the table and convince her to really give this marriage a try. He knew in his heart that he could make her happy. He had known it for years.

But if she still needed time, he was more than willing to give her as much of it as she needed.

He arrived at her penthouse at the Beverly Hilton. She tried to just hop out of the car and grab her own bags, but Ram wasn't having any of that. He parked and insisted on bringing his wife's luggage up to her penthouse.

"That's not necessary," she insisted.

"Oh it is necessary. And besides, I *want* to do it." When she folded her arms, he added, "You need to get used to letting a man take care of you."

He placed a finger against her mouth before she could say anything to argue with him. "I'm not talking about financially. I'm talking about emotionally." Their eyes locked. "Everyone needs someone to love and to hold. Someone to share their darkest secrets with. To laugh and play with." He reached up and cupped the side of her face. "You know—how we used to do."

Sofia stared into Ramell's eyes and was instantly transported back to a time when she trusted him with all her secrets, a time when she knew without a doubt that one day they would be together forever. That moment in time now felt like it was yesterday. And in many ways, he was the same Ram, waiting on her to hand him her heart.

"You love me," she said. It wasn't a question.

He smiled. "I have *always* loved you." He leaned down and slowly drew her lips into a kiss. It started off soft and slow but it quickly heated up to the point that their mouths delved into each others like they were completely ravenous for one another.

The next thing Sofia knew she was sliding her arms up

around his neck so that she could pull him closer. Yes, he tasted like chocolate, and yes, he was the most addictive thing she'd ever known, but most importantly, he tasted like love. Sweet, heady, and completely intoxicating. Now that she recognized the taste it consumed her and knocked down walls that she never even knew she had erected. When she managed to pull their lips apart, her chest heaved like she had just traveled the entire world in less than sixty seconds.

Ram's devilish smile slid into place. "Now may I help take your bags up to your penthouse, Mrs. Jordan?"

Hell. She forgot that they were still standing in the parking deck. What happened to her hatred of public displays of affection? "Yeah. That would be nice."

"Good." He kissed the tip of her nose. "I kind of like convincing you to see things my way." Ram grabbed her bags from the trunk and when they turned to head toward the building, Sofia's sister stood there smiling.

"Rachel." Sofia blinked. "What are you doing here?"

"What else? I came to see you." Rachel walked over to her older sister and drew her into a hug. "The last time we talked I think it's safe to say that you were a little... out of it."

Sofia laughed. "That's putting it nicely." She kissed her sister's cheek before she pulled out of her arms.

"But after seeing that kiss, I know now that there's absolutely nothing to worry about." Rachel turned toward Ramell. "And I guess that makes you my new brother-in-law," Rachel said, sweeping her arms open wide.

Ram lowered Sofia's luggage and quickly embraced

Rachel in a hug. "Hey, I always wanted a little sister." And just like that the two clicked. They had always known each other, but the recent marriage made them instant best friends. Ramell retrieved the bags and together all three of them walked up to Sofia's penthouse.

When they entered the luxurious apartment, Ram asked where the bedroom was and Sofia hesitated. She had another jolt of everything moving so fast, but then shook it off to show him the way. Rachel stayed in the living room to give them a few minutes of privacy.

In the bedroom, Ram set her bags on the bed and took a look around her peach and gold bedroom. "Nice."

"Thank you."

"It's not as nice as mine, of course, but it's nice."

"We're having a contest now?"

"I'm just saying." He shrugged his shoulders. He walked over to her and swung his arms around her waist. "Make sure when I come and pick you up tomorrow that you pack enough clothes to stay at my house for a while."

She drew in a deep breath.

"I have more than one bedroom you know. There's no pressure."

Sofia flashed the simple band around her fingers. "No. There's just a wedding band."

"Hey," he said with a sudden note of seriousness. "You know me. I'll wait as long as you need me to."

She did know that; had known it for a long time. "Thank you," she whispered.

"No. Thank you."

"For what?"

"For finally asking *me* to marry *you*."

Chapter 12

The next morning, Sofia strolled through the office doors of Limelight Entertainment Management wearing a big smile. Almost everyone she passed in the building seemed to go out of their way to stop and offer their congratulations and well wishes. Sure, there was one or two of them that pointed or snickered about the Elvis impersonator or the small clip of Ramell giving her a strip dance—which, had, incidentally, generated hundreds of thousands of views online.

But none of that bothered her. She was too excited about her date tonight. Not even Stewart, who had screwed up her coffee order and dropped a very important director's call four times in a row, could upset her. It turned out she wasn't on her A-game, either. While Larry Franklin was still trying to lowball her on Ethan's next contract, her mind was still trying to figure out what she was going to wear that evening. When she left for work that morning, she had narrowed her selection down to seven dresses.

"Sofia, are you still there?"

"Huh, what?" She blinked out of her stupor.

Larry cleared his throat. "I'm sorry. Was I boring you?"

"No." She started to apologize but stopped. "But I'm still disappointed in the offer." Sofia had no idea what he'd offered, but it was her job to press for more anyway so her answer couldn't have been wrong.

"All right, all right. I give. We'll accept your last counteroffer. Does that make you happy?"

She perked up. "Extremely."

"I'll have legal draw up the contracts," Larry huffed, and she could tell that he was lighting one of his favorite illegal Cuban cigars. "I have to tell you, Sofia, I had hoped that marriage would have softened you a little."

"There you go thinking again, Larry. I told you that was a dangerous proposition." They shared a brief laugh and then ended their call. A second later, Uncle Jacob knocked on Sofia's glass door. She glanced up and smiled. "It's about time you rolled in," she said, glancing at her watch.

"Actually, it's my day off. I only came in to see you," he said, strolling over to her desk. "Two days after your nuptials and you're already back to work? I was hoping that marriage would've curbed some of your workaholic ways."

"Seems everyone has been hoping that marriage would change me," she said, a little irritated at that discovery.

Uncle Jacob's kind face crinkled at the corners. "Not change you. I just want you to slow down and smell the roses." He moved around her desk and opened his arms. "In my eyes, you and your sister are perfect."

Sofia stood and embraced her uncle. Because he was her father's twin, it had always been easy to view him as both her uncle and her father. With him around, she could never forget her father's face. And when she wanted to see her mother all she had to do was look in the mirror.

"I come bearing news of your wedding reception," he said after they had exchanged a long hug.

"The wedding reception." Sofia sank back into her chair. "You know Aunt Lily really doesn't have to go through any trouble. In fact, I'm sure that she has to be up to her eyeballs helping Rachel plan her wedding."

"Nonsense. We want to celebrate both of your unions." His smile doubled in size as his gaze started to shimmer with tears. "I know that your parents have to be smiling down on you two right now. I've only met Ethan a couple of times but I know that he and your sister are going to be happy for a long, long time. And as for you." He reached down and tweaked her nose. "I've known for a very long time how Ramell has felt about you. I don't think anyone who has ever been in the same room with you two didn't know that one day…" He waved his finger and then winked.

Sofia smiled but dropped her gaze.

"But how do you feel about him," Jacob asked. "Do you love him?"

She took her time thinking the question over. She

thought about the years that she had foolishly blamed Ram for the things his father did. It had been unfair, but at the time it was the only way she knew how to cope.

"Sofia?" Jacob pressed, concern starting to seep into his voice.

"I think I've always loved him…in some way," she finally said. "Given how I've treated him, I'm not sure that I deserve him."

Jacob chuckled. "We all deserve love, Sofia. Don't you ever forget that."

She nodded and let his words wash over her.

"As for your reception, it's next Friday and then the week after that we all head out to Napa Valley for Rachel's wedding and for Thanksgiving."

"Next Friday?"

"It was going to be sooner than that but Emmett is out in New York and won't be back until that Wednesday so we settled on Friday."

Sofia's hands tightened on the pen in her hand. "She's inviting Emmett?"

Jacob paused and then said softly, "Well he is Ramell's father. It only seems right to invite him to the wedding reception."

Sofia clenched her teeth together in order to prevent herself from saying something nasty. But the effort was hard and it instantly brought on a headache.

Jacob watched her reaction and then seemed to struggle with something. "Sofia, maybe it's time we had a little talk about Emmett Jordan," he started, propping a hip up on her desk.

"No," she said sternly. "The last thing I want to do is talk about that man."

"But—"

"I mean it," she snapped, feeling her face heat up. In the brief three days she had to think about this marriage, she hadn't given much thought on how she was going to have to handle *him* being her new father-in-law. The only solution that popped in her head right now was to keep the same game plan that she'd always had: stay the hell away from him.

"Well thank you, Uncle Jacob. I'll definitely tell Ramell our schedule."

Uncle Jacob's brows hiked up. "He's not here? You left him home alone?"

"Actually, he mentioned something about needing the day off to plan for our first date."

Jacob laughed. "Well, in that case I guess it's all right. You have any idea what he has in mind?"

"None." She thought about it. "Maybe I should be worried?"

"Or," Jacob said, standing again, "maybe you should be excited."

Sofia didn't work a full day, something that should have been marked in the history books. Instead, she begged for her favorite hairdresser to fit her in. After that it was a rushed manicure and pedicure and then an eyebrow threading before racing back to her penthouse to decide on what to wear.

"What happened to my other Prada shoe?" she wondered aloud while she searched her bags. After another twenty-minute search, she gave up and went for her black Jimmy Choos and a black Chanel dress.

Their date was for eight o'clock and that was exactly when her door bell rang. She gave herself a last casual glance in the mirror and went to answer the door. She started off with a casual stroll, but when the bell rang a second time, she ended up doing a light jog to the front door.

When she opened it, Ram stood on the other side in a black suit with one hand in his pocket and the other one mysteriously behind his back. "Good evening, Mrs. Jordan."

That wonderful feeling of warmth rushed through her body again. Once again, Ram looked good from head to toe and she had to force herself to stop staring. "Evening."

"Mind if I come in?"

She stepped back with a smile. "Absolutely. Come in."

When he strolled through the door, his signature cologne filled her senses and weakened her knees. His white smile and kissable lips had her heart tripping in her chest. When on earth had he learned to turn her on so quickly? "I brought something for you," he said.

"Oh?" She closed the door behind him.

Ramell gently pulled out a bundle of daisies. "I didn't think I'd be able to find them in November," he admitted.

Tears stung the back of her eyes while her smile tripled in size. "My favorite."

"I know." He stepped closer and tipped her chin. "I

remember." His head slowly descended until their lips locked together. His broad chest felt wonderful pressed against her. Her heartbeat became erratic. If this was all that he had planned, then he wouldn't get any complaints from her.

This is crazy. But despite that, she was willing to see where this wild and unexpected ride was going to lead her. *Everyone deserves love.*

Ram pulled back and then kissed the tip of her nose. "Are you ready to go?"

Not sure that she could speak, she nodded. But when she tried to walk, she still wobbled a bit. *What on earth is this man doing to me?*

"Where are your bags?"

"Uh. I haven't actually had a chance to pack yet," she informed him, looking for a vase that would fit her short stemmed bouquet. "It took all of my free time just to get ready."

His gaze roamed over her again. "Don't worry about it. It was worth every second." He offered her his arm and then escorted her out of the penthouse.

"Am I allowed to know where we're going now?" she asked when he opened the passenger-side door of his car for her.

"No." He tossed her a wink and then shut the door. A few minutes later they were on the road and cruising down the highway.

When it became clear where Ram was taking her, a fresh wave of tears filled her eyes. "I don't believe it."

Ram reached over, took her hand and kissed it. "Are you upset?"

Sofia shook her head as she stared at her old childhood home. The white three-story mansion nestled on a grassy knoll looked exactly as she had remembered. In a lot of ways it was as if time had just stood still. For years she kept promising herself to come by the old estate, but always allowed herself to get caught up with work or some other social function. A part of her also believed that the memories would be too painful, but now that she was standing there she couldn't stop smiling. Only belatedly did she realize that the lights were still on.

"Does someone live here?"

"Not exactly." Ram climbed out of the car and rushed to the other side to help her out.

Taking his hand, Sofia looked up into Ram's soulful eyes and felt like she was stepping out of his car and into a dream. Again, she wondered at the magic he seemed to be able to cast over her at will. How she had been able to fight it as long as she had would probably be a mystery to her for the rest of her life. But right now, at this moment, she just allowed it to consume her.

"Our table awaits," he said.

Sofia cocked a curious smile, but floated along beside him as he escorted her around the house. Once they made it to the backyard her gaze immediately zoomed to the large oak tree where she and Ramell used to steal childhood kisses. Tonight, a round linen-covered table with two flickering candles sat beneath it. Next to it a singular waiter and a violinist awaited them.

"Oh my God." Sofia clutched a hand over her heart and a fresh wave of tears threatened to ruin her makeup.

She glanced to her left and met Ram's gaze again. "It's beautiful."

"Believe me, it pales next to you." He leaned over for another kiss. Each time he did it was as if heaven had momentarily touched down on earth. When their lips pulled apart, he escorted her the rest of the way to their waiting table. He'd pulled a few strings to get Patina to cater this evening. It was Sofia's favorite restaurant according to her sister. And he made sure to have her favorite meal prepared. "I can't believe that you went through all this trouble," she said as he pulled out her chair.

"It was no trouble at all. I wanted to do this." When she sat, he brushed his lips lightly against her shoulders. When her soft skin trembled beneath his touch, his chest swelled with love and his confidence soared. He took his seat and allowed the stirring music from the violin and the evening's cool breeze to wrap around them while their waiter busied himself removing their silver trays.

"You're quite the romantic," Sofia said, blushing.

"I hope you don't mind."

She shrugged shyly. "I guess there are worse things in the world."

Ram couldn't stop looking at her. He could sit there all night watching the evening's gentle breeze play with her hair. Between the candlelight and the moonlight, she looked like she'd just descended from heaven.

"Stop." She shook her head, looking uncharacteristically shy.

"Stop what?"

"Stop looking at me like that."

He laughed. "And just how am I looking at you?"

Her cheeks stained red as she shook her head. "You're making me self-conscious."

"I'm sorry, but I can't help it. I've never had a wife before."

Her eyes met his again, but something flickered in them that scared him for a moment. "What is it?" he asked, wanting to tackle any problem head on.

"Well, I guess…I'm wondering, what are we doing? It's not like we really meant to get married, right?"

The question shaved a few inches off of his smile.

"I mean when I started receiving all those calls and Uncle Jacob seemed so happy…I couldn't bring myself to tell them…"

"Tell them what?" his voice dropped as he prepared for her to say something that was going to tear him apart.

"I couldn't tell them the truth."

He sat silently during a few bars from the violin before he could bring himself to ask. "And what is the truth, Sofia?"

Her eyes started shimmering with tears while she tried to find the right words. "That's just it. Our truth is complicated."

He breathed a sigh of relief. "Not on my end." Ram reached across the table and took her hand. "My truth is that I'm thrilled that we're married. I love that you have my last name because I have loved you my whole life. And I have a sneaking suspicion that you feel the same way about me. I just never understood why you insisted on fighting it."

In a flash, Sofia remembered poking her head into her father's study and seeing him enraged and yelling and hurling accusations at Ram's father. A lump swelled in the center of her throat while her gaze lowered to where his hand held hers. Their fingers looked so perfect entwined together. "It's so complicated."

"So complicated that you can't even tell me?"

The only other person Sofia had ever shared what she'd seen and heard that night with was her sister, Rachel. And now her new husband was asking and she didn't know how to go about repeating those words to him. It was his father, after all, and as far as she knew they were very close.

"You know…maybe it's just best to kind of leave it in the past," she decided. "Tonight…we should be celebrating our first date," she chuckled, hoping to lighten the mood.

He smiled. "Moving forward, I guess what I need to know is whether we're seriously going to give this marriage a try—or is this some kind of charade we're just putting on for family and friends because…what? Because we don't know how to tell them that we got drunk and did something wild and spontaneous?"

She blinked.

"Do you want an annulment?" he asked. "Tell me now because I don't do charades." And there it was. His cards laid out on the table.

Sofia drew a deep breath while her head started to spin.

"It simple," he said. "Do you want to stay married to me?"

Chapter 13

In an instant Sofia was transported back to that last time they were in this backyard, Ramell standing in front of her with a bundle of wild daisies and asking her if she would marry him. And just like then, her stomach filled with butterflies while her heart skipped around in her chest. He stared at her with the same intensity, the same confidence and the same amount of love.

"I honestly don't know," she whispered and then slowly bobbed her head. "I guess we could give it a try—for the time being."

Ram tossed down his linen napkin and jumped up from the table. He walked over to Sofia's seat, pulled her up and crushed his mouth against hers. Holding any stream of conscious thought was impossible so she didn't even bother to try. She just floated around in an endless abyss of desire.

"You don't know how happy you just made me," he whispered, coming up for air. "I've waited my whole life to hear you say those words…soberly." They laughed while he continued to cup her face. "I promise you that you won't regret this." He kissed her again and swirled her in time to the music.

"I have another surprise for you," Ram said softly.

Sofia pulled back. "Really? I don't know if my heart can take any more surprises."

"Just one more." He gently turned her around so that she faced the back of her old home. "I was thinking about that conversation we had about whether we should live at your place or mine."

"I thought you said—"

"I bought this house," he announced.

Sofia's mouth opened and remained like that for a long moment before she finally asked, "What?"

"I bought this house today." He lowered his arms to her waist while he waited for her response. At the sound of a soft sniffle, he jerked toward her. "I'm sorry. I didn't mean to upset you."

Shaking her head, Sofia placed a hand over her mouth while silent tears rolled down her face.

"We don't have to move here," Ram said, desperate to fix the situation. "My place is fine. Or we can live at your place. I don't care. I'll live wherever you want to live."

Sofia spun toward him and wrapped her arms around his neck. "No. It's okay. I love it. It's just so overwhelming. Thank you." She sobbed gently against his chest before lifting her head up and receiving the kiss she sought. This time her lips were salted with tears.

"Would you like to go inside?" he asked.

She quickly nodded and then grasped his hand before they took off in the direction of the back doors. Of course none of the old furniture was there, but the house still felt like home with the rented modern furniture. "It's so… perfect."

They strolled through the house while recalling different childhood stories. Like when they used to make chocolate chip cookies or colored Easter eggs with Sofia's mother. Upstairs, she stopped at what used to be Rachel's baby room and then her room. She touched the walls where her mother used to mark how tall she was growing.

"I don't know why I haven't visited this house more often," she whispered, shaking her head. "I kept telling myself I would but…"

"Too busy?"

She glanced over at him. "No lectures this evening."

He surrendered by tossing up his hands. "Agreed."

They continued their stroll until they reached the master bedroom. Sofia's heart contracted because she remembered so many nights that she had run to this room for the comfort of her father's arms to protect her from bad storms or nightmares. But like the rest of the house, her parents' old furniture was gone and in its place a California King postal bed with royal blue silk sheets sat like a regal throne toward the back of the room. She stepped further into the room while Ramell hung back.

Sofia glanced at the walls, the windows, the crown

molding—but her gaze kept creeping toward the bed. "Can I ask you a question?"

Ramell cleared his throat. "Of course you can."

"It's about our, um, wedding night."

"All right." He leaned against the doorframe. "I hope I can help."

"Do you know whether we...you know?"

His brows hiked while a different kind of smile inched across his lips. "Did we make love?"

"Well...I know that you said something about first and second base."

"Don't forget about third," he said.

Sofia swallowed. "Remind me what third base is again."

Within the blink of an eye, the flirtation in his gaze transformed into something primal—hungry. "Third base is when I lay you down and start kissing you from the heel of your foot, up to the back of your calf—where you're ticklish by the way—then up the inside of your thighs. I watch you quiver for a while and then I travel further up while I peel your panties from your hips and then spread you legs open so I can...enjoy the taste of your inner beauty."

Hit with a sudden heat wave, Sofia's knees started to wobble. Her mind had replayed the images in her head while he talked. "So it wasn't a dream," she whispered.

Ram locked gazes as he shook his head. "No. It was paradise."

She licked her lips. "Can you take me there again?"

With a moan, he strolled across the room. When their

bodies connected, he was fire to her dynamite. Sofia felt as if she was being devoured. Ram's hot mouth latched on to her pearled nipples while his large hands spread her silken legs open. She tilted her head back as far she could against the pillows in hopes of tugging in a few streams of oxygen. It worked for a few seconds but then she decided to take her chances with the fire by leaning forward so she could rain kisses against the top of Ram's head.

He continued to nibble and suck while slowly working a finger through the soft, wet V between her legs.

"Oooooh," Sofia sighed and lifted her hips to allow Ram to slide a second finger into her smooth flesh. Her world spun as he rotated his fingers until he could hear her body's juices start to make smacking noises. By then his head was directly over her soft springy curls and he wasted no time unrolling his long tongue to taste the honey within.

Melodic moans rolled off of Sofia's lips and seemed to blend effortlessly with the violin that still played outside their window. She closed her eyes, surprised by just how much her body was trembling. It was like an earthquake that didn't have an end in sight. She gave up her quest for oxygen and welcomed the idea of death by pleasure as her first orgasm started to churn at the base of her body.

Unbelievably, Ramell's tongue sank deeper, hitting the G-spot that supplied all her body's honey. His tongue flicked, rotated and flicked again, causing Sofia to clamp her hands around Ram's head. She was both pushing him away and locking him in place at the same time.

Then, an explosion. She tried to scream out but her voice failed. Her toes balled like fists and her knees squeezed Ram's head like a nutcracker. While waves of euphoria washed over her, Ram struggled to pry her legs back open. When he finally succeeded, he climbed back up her body and chuckled against her neck. "Remind me to strap you down next time."

Before her aftershocks had fully subsided, Ram brought her back to the brink again by working in one, two and then three fingers into her slick honey pot.

When she started to thrash again, Ram's mouth made its way back to her breasts. "Oooh, Ram," she recited. Each time she said his name, he picked up the pace until his entire hand was as wet as she was.

The pleasure was too much, too intense. Just when her second orgasm was about to slam into her, she lifted her hips high to give Ram better access. Next thing she knew she was hitting her head hard against the headboard and trying to escape Ram's wicked fingers. "Wait. Please," she begged. "I need to catch my breath."

"Is that right?"

Panting, Sofia could tell that his ego was swelling out of control. She put on her best sexy smile and then brushed his hands from between her legs. "All right, Mr. Jordan. Your head game is on point." She rolled him onto his back. "But you're not the only one with skills, you know."

Ramell laughed. "Careful now. The last time you started bragging, you left a brother hanging."

Sofia frowned. "What?"

"You fell asleep kissing my stomach."

Embarrassment heated her face. "No. I didn't."

"I'm afraid so." He laughed and drew her in for a kiss. "It's okay, baby. The kissing was nice. The cold shower was another story."

She pushed him back down onto the bed. "Well, there won't be any cold showers tonight." Sofia climbed on top and straddled Ram's trim hips. Gazing down at him, he looked like a chocolate deity and she definitely had a sweet tooth. Lowering her head, Sofia slowly and deliberately ran her tongue over his chest.

"Ooh. Now that's nice," he said, folding his hands behind his head so he could watch her work her magic. And it was a sort of magic, that the way his body tingled wherever her tongue roamed. When she glazed over one of his hard nipples, a thin sigh seeped out of his chest and he grew even harder.

Sofia floated down his body like a feather. For a brief moment her open legs and pink pearl brushed against his iron-hard erection, and despite the momentary pleasure, she kept moving down until his thick and mountainous length stood tall before her face.

"Oh my goodness," she moaned, staring in awe. Curious, she wrapped one hand around him and smiled when she saw that her fingers just barely made it around the base.

"You sure you know what you're doing down there, sweetheart?"

Sofia's brows jumped at the challenge. She immediately rolled out her tongue and then slowly dragged it up and then down his straining flesh. The muscle quivered and jumped. When it did, it bounced against Sofia's lips.

Laughing, she tried again. Her tongue went up and down, soliciting a moan and then a hiss from Ramell. To push him over the edge, she opened and relaxed her jaw so she could sink her mouth over the fat, mushroom-shaped head. She sank down as far as she could, held him and then squeezed the muscles in the back of her throat.

Ram called out to the Almighty and then raked his fingers through her long hair.

She released him, bobbed her head up and then sank back down before he had a chance to catch his breath. He hissed, groaned and then latched his hand on the back of her head as she now set a steady but maddening pace. Periodically she would stop, squeeze and then bob again.

Words of love, lust and a few things in between tumbled out of his mouth. Chances were he didn't know what he was saying. And now that the shoe was on the other foot, he was having a hard time trying to lie still. He was going to come and he didn't want that.

"Okay, baby. You can stop," he half begged while he attempted to pull her up.

She warded off his hands for as long as she could, but when it was clear that he was seconds from exploding, Ram reached down and pried her off of him. Sofia came away laughing.

"Ah. So you think that's funny?" He pinned her beneath him and then smothered kisses against the crook of her neck while his wet erection slapped against her core. "I know how to make you serious," he said.

"Do you now?" She giggled and squirmed.

"Uh-huh," he said seductively, his hardness rubbing

against her spot without his help. "Now that I have educated you about reaching third base, what do you say we take this on home?"

Instead of answering, Sofia reached down in between their bodies and grabbed hold of him and guided him directly into her silky walls. It was a bold maneuver, but the minute Ram started to sink into her body, her eyes widened and her body started to tense at his length and width. The combination of pain and pleasure caused pearl-size tears to form and roll from the corners of her eyes.

Ram stopped. "Are you okay, baby? You need me to stop?"

"No. Please. Don't stop," she panted, rolling her hands around his waist and urging his hips to sink lower.

He curled his body so that he could kiss the tracks of her tears while still submerging deeper. The pleasure of feeling her vaginal muscles pulse in time with her heartbeat had Ram's mind spinning like a pinwheel. Breathing became a chore while he fought for control. If he started moving too soon, he risked becoming a two-minute brother and that would be one hell of a way to start off his marriage.

Luckily, Sofia was still trying to adjust to his size, so together they had an undeclared time out. Soon enough the kissing returned and Ram started to rock her slow and deep. Sighing, she thrust her head back and then lifted her legs to wrap them around his trim waist. Together they found a rhythm and lost themselves in the splendor of each other.

Euphoric, Sofia alternated between calling out for

God and Ramell. Tears of joy continued to roll down her face.

"Do you love me, Sofia?" Ram asked, his hips now a human drill.

"Y-yes," she cried. "Oh, yes."

"Then I want to hear you say it, baby."

"I—I love you, Ram baby."

"I love you, too." He dropped his head lower, sucked in a nipple and hammered and licked until his ears rang with her screaming his name. He hiked her legs higher and enjoyed the sound of their bodies slapping together. At long last an orgasmic cry seemed to tear from her very soul while her mind spun into sweet oblivion. Two deep strokes later, Ram growled and clenched a large fistful of the bedding while he exploded inside of her.

For long minutes afterward, neither one of them could speak. They just lay there, hot and sweaty, clinging to each other. The sound of the violin was still playing somewhere off in the distance. They both seemed to realize that at the same time.

"That dude is working for his money," Ram laughed, climbing out of the large bed.

When he rushed over to the window, Sofia rolled onto her side and ogled his perfect behind and low-swinging manhood. She smiled at the knowledge that he now belonged to her. She belonged to him. They belonged together.

Ram opened the window and let out a loud whistle. "Yo, man. You can head out."

The music finally stopped and Sofia snickered and shook her head. "How long has he been out there?"

"I don't know." Ram glanced at his watch. "Wow. It's one in the morning."

"No!"

He bobbed his head as he headed back over to the bed. Once there, he grabbed her and pulled her close. Their bodies snapped together like two missing pieces of a puzzle. However, before he could get round two started, Sofia's stomach growled like a starved lion.

She gasped and then covered her face in embarrassment.

"I take it that means you're hungry," Ram laughed.

"Well, we never did have dinner and we did burn up quite a lot of calories," she reminded him.

"Then let's see what we can do about that." He kissed her on her collarbone and then climbed back out of bed. After a quick shower together where they played just a little more than they concentrated on getting clean, they were left having to wrap their wet bodies in clean sheets instead of drying off with towels because they couldn't find any. When they descended the large staircase, they looked like a college couple about to attend a toga party.

The surprise was seeing that their waiter had moved their outdoor dinner party back into the house. Sure they had to remove it from the refrigerator and heat everything up in the microwave, but it was still food for the starving husband and wife. For the next hour they laughed and reminisced about a time long gone. It felt good opening up to one another. To Sofia, it even felt like she had her best friend back.

It was perfect.
Almost too perfect.
Surely, a shoe had to drop.

Chapter 14

Sofia woke with the sound of birds chirping outside of her window. She sighed, smiled and tried to snuggle closer to the muscled body lying next to her. If she could carry a tune she might've just busted out singing "I'm Every Woman."

"So how long are you going to lay there and pretend that you're asleep?" Ramell asked.

Sofia's smile stretched wider as she fluttered her eyes open. "I thought that *you* were asleep."

"Are you kidding me? We've been waiting a couple of hours for you to wake up."

"We?"

Ram nodded downward and Sofia's gaze followed its direction to see her husband's early morning erection. "Oh my." She arched a brow and reflexively licked her lips. "Is this something I can look forward to every morning?" She reached down and slowly pulled the top sheet until it slid off of Ram's impeccably chiseled body. His length stood straight up like a black obelisk.

"I hope that's not a problem," Ramell said, cupping her chin with his fingers and then tilting it upward so he could have his first kiss of the day. The first brush of his lips was sweet but then when his tongue swept inside her mouth a familiar heat rushed up her body and pure passion took over.

Before she knew it, she was swinging her leg across his waist while he sat up in bed so he could stretch his hot mouth over her full breasts. Sofia was as wet as he was hard and it made it easy for him to enter her quickly and thoroughly. Sofia smiled and rolled her hips in a figure eight so that Ram's steel rod could hit her four walls perfectly and caused a few sighs to blend with her moans. They were going at it like they had been lovers all of their lives. She arched her back further until she could grab hold of his ankles. Honey gushed between her legs with each grind and thrust, caused their bodies to make loud, exotic popping and squishing noises.

"That's it, baby. That's it." Ram skimmed his fingers down the front of her body and then dipped them in between the wet folds of her lips and she thumped back against the pads of his fingertips.

"Oh. You feel good, baby," he praised. "So damn good."

"Yeah? You like that?" she asked.

"You know that I do," he panted.

"Well, I have something else for you," she said. Sofia maneuvered and turned around with their bodies still connected. Her knees remained on both sides of his hips, her legs curled behind his back while she lay down in between the V of his legs. Then she started to grind.

And Ram lost his mind.

He watched the incredible sight of her perfect round ass while it bounced, flexed and rotated until his toes started to tingle. "Oh damn." Ram parted her cheeks so he could watch as he flowed in and out of her to the precise rhythm that was playing inside his head.

Sofia panted, thrashing her head from side to side, but still working her hips, pelvis and vaginal muscles so that there was no mistake as to who was in control. "You feel so good."

Not as good as you feel. He closed his eyes for a second and bit his lower lip when the pleasure intensified. *It should be a crime for anything to feel this good.* Then again, if it was a crime then he would just have to get locked up. Ram would risk anything and everything for mornings like this.

Sofia practically hissed as her vaginal muscles tightened. The next thing she knew, her moans skipped up the musical scale until she hit a high C. When the beginnings of her first morning orgasm stirred in her belly, everything started to tremble like she was a human earthquake.

"Are you about to come?" Ram asked, locking his hands down on her hips.

Sofia tried to answer, but all she could manage was a few more moans.

Ram was glad to hear it. He was close too and he didn't want to blast off before she did. A few more rolls of her hips and Sofia cried in ecstasy. Ram followed shortly after, growling with pleasure upon the intensity of his release.

Spent, Ram fell back onto the bed's pillows like a chopped tree. Sofia chuckled and struggled to get her feet from beneath him. He didn't help because he couldn't. She had sapped every drop of energy out of him, but he was happy and satisfied. "I could die a happy man right now."

Sofia chuckled while she still lazily rolled her hips.

"What are you doing to me?"

Ram hitched up one side of his face while he slid his hands all around her beautiful brown behind. "If you're trying to get a brother to fall in love with you then you can quit. That happened a long time ago."

Sofia pushed herself up and spread her legs out until she had the perfect cheerleader split over his still hard erection. "Then maybe I just want to make sure that you stay that way."

"You weren't playing when you said that you had tricks." He sat back up and wrapped an arm around her waist while he scooted over to the edge of the bed and then stood up with their bodies still joined.

"What are you about to do?" Sofia asked, laughing.

"You'll see," he chuckled. "Plant your feet on the floor."

She did as she was told while he turned so that she leaned over the bed. From there he took hold of her arms held them up from behind her like they were a pair of reins and then started thrusting his hips. Each time he would slap against her lovely bottom, she would bounce forward but his tight hold on her arms prevented her from falling onto the bed and ensured her springing back for another hard thrust.

"Ohh." Sofia's mouth sagged open while a new wave of ecstasy washed over her. She dropped her head and then watched as her full breasts bounced and jiggled while the friction from their bodies soon had her weak in the knees. More importantly, her muscles started to tighten, and caused Ramell to moan her name.

"Kiss me," he said, holding still long enough to release her hands so she could erect her top half and turn her face over her left shoulder to receive his hungry kiss. While their mouths caressed and their tongues dueled, Ram eased a hand down the front of her body where his fingers slithered through her dewy curls. Feeling her quiver and swallowing her moans, Ram rotated his hips and gently massaged her core.

In need of oxygen, Sofia broke their kiss to suck in deep gulps of air. Ram's lips found a new home against the curve of her neck. Before she knew it, she was popping off orgasms back to back, followed again by Ram's release. When they finally fell onto the bed, they were laughing and gasping for air. Neither of them were sure who went to sleep first, but when they woke again, Ram joked, "We're really late for work."

"Work?" Sofia sprung up. "Oh my God, what time is it?"

"Huh, what?" Before he could process what was happening, Sofia had bolted out of bed and slammed the door to the bathroom and he could hear her turning on the shower. "Wait. Come back." He rolled out of bed, peeked at his watch and went after her.

In the bathroom, he opened the glass stall and walked inside. "Here, let me help you," he offered, reaching for the soap.

"Only if you're really going to help and not try to distract me. I need to get to the office."

"Why?" he laughed. "It's already past noon. We might as well go ahead and take the day off."

Sofia stopped scrubbing beneath her breasts to stare at him as if he'd lost all his marbles. "Take the day off?"

Ramell hiked up a brow. "What? You have taken a day off before, haven't you?"

"I've taken vacation before, yes, but it's been a while."

Now it was his turn to lower the soap and stare at her as if she'd just sprouted a second head. "You've never played hooky from work before?"

"And why would I want to do that?"

"Because it's fun?" He shrugged his mountainous shoulders.

She shook her head and rolled her eyes. "No. I actually take my work seriously."

"Well not today," he said, turning her around and soaping down her back. "Today you and me are going to play hooky."

"What? Are you kidding me? I probably have like…a million emails and phone messages by now."

"They can wait until tomorrow," Ram said. "And don't bother to argue with me. I'm not going to take no for an answer."

She did argue, but in the end he won.

* * *

After their shower, they returned to Sofia's penthouse so she could change clothes. "How casual are we talking about?" Sofia asked.

Ramell followed her into her bedroom. Upon seeing the queen-size bed, he instantly dove on top of it. "You know before you move out we're going to have to test the springs on this one."

She turned and settled her hands on her hips. "And why is that?"

"Because it's a bed. Do we really need another reason?"

"You're insatiable."

"And that's a bad thing?"

Sofia held her hand up and gave him the brick wall. "I'm ignoring you."

Ramell laughed. "Whatever. Just grab some jeans and a shirt. Nothing fancy."

"Uh-huh. You still haven't told me where we're going," Sofia said, pulling out a pair of Chip and Pepper jeans. "I think I have the right to know where you're dragging me off to."

"Dragging? I offer you a day of fun and leisure and you call that dragging you?"

"Tell me where we're going and let me be the judge of whether it's going to be fun and leisure."

"No." He climbed off of the bed. "You'll say no so you can run back to your precious little office where you can listen to actors and directors whine, or so that you can fleece more money out of studio executives."

"What can I say? Work is my spice of life."

Ramell shook his head as he moved over to his wife and pulled her into his arms. "Not anymore. Now I'm the *new* spice in your life." He leaned forward and nibbled on her ear. "Just like you're the new spice in mine."

Sofia wanted to pretend that his warm breath against her skin wasn't affecting her, but her moans slipped out before she had the chance to stop it.

"You know we can try that bed out now instead of later."

"I knew it. You don't really have anything planned for today."

"We just decided to play hooky an hour ago—and yes, I know where I'm taking you."

"Then tell me."

Ramell shook his head and then smacked her on the behind. "Change your clothes. I'll wait for you in the living room. If I see naked skin then we'll never get out of here."

"Oh really?" Sofia slid the straps of her dress off of her shoulders.

Ramell quickly slammed his eyes shut and then turned away to feel his way out of the room. "I will not be tempted," he said as he made his way out. "Just hurry up so we can go."

Sofia laughed as she watched him being silly. Again, it felt good to just be able to laugh and play the way they used to do. All those wasted years of holding that damn grudge while she and Ramell could've… She stopped. Could've what?

Her gaze fell to the small wedding band on her right hand and she knew the answer to that. How many times had Ramell proposed when they were children? How many times had she wanted to say yes, but played hard to get because that was what her mother had coached her to do?

Then, just as quickly as it came, Sofia dismissed the thought. They were just children. There was no way of knowing whether their puppy love would have survived elementary school, let alone junior high and high school. The odds of that happening had to be something like a million to one. Or a gazillion to one, she corrected herself. She laughed softly and then went back into her closet for a pair of Nikes.

When she emerged from her bedroom, she found Ramell in the kitchen rinsing off some strawberries. "Hmm. You know a man in the kitchen is like an aphrodisiac to a woman."

"Why the hell do you think I'm in here for?" He held up a strawberry and then watched her hungrily as she took her sweet time opening her mouth and sliding it in tip first.

"You're a damn tease is what you are," Ram said, plopping the red fruit into her mouth and stepping back. "But I'm onto you. Are you ready to go?"

Sofia reached over to the fruit bowl and picked up a banana. "I'm dressed, if that's what you mean." She took her time peeling the fruit.

Ram watched, completely fascinated, as she then tilted the banana toward her mouth. This time her tongue performed a little dance that involved licking and swirling her tongue around the tip. By the time she took a healthy bite, he was rock hard and was seconds away from grabbing her and spreading her out on the counter for a different kind of meal.

Instead, he pushed the fruit aside, took her by the hand and led her toward the front door.

Sofia laughed. "Is there a problem?"

"Yeah. You play too much."

"I thought there was no such thing as playing too much?" Sofia said with a wink, tossing his words back at him.

"Oh wait, wait." She stopped and started back toward the bedroom.

Ramell tossed up his hands. "What is it now?"

"My cell phone. I need to grab my cell phone off the charger."

"Oh, no." He rushed after her and grabbed her hand again. "No cell phones. No computers. No gadgets of any kind."

"But—"

"And no buts. We're playing hooky, remember?" He started dragging her toward the door. "Hooky means no work."

"I don't know if I like hooky," she said, poking out her bottom lip.

Ramell opened the front door and smiled. "You say that now, but trust me, you're going to forget all about that phone soon enough."

Chapter 15

They played hooky at Venice Beach. Blue ocean and an azure sky, it was like most of California—beautiful year round and always crowded. There were a ton of things to do. There were several vendors selling crafts, drawings and every type of junk food one could imagine. But it was the street performers that really caught their attention and entertained them.

At the Sidewalk Café, Ram and Sofia grabbed a light lunch and had fun checking out the eclectic crowd. Clearly mohawks were making a comeback. As well as spandex.

"Now you know I want to get you on some skates," Ram said, munching on some hot wings.

"Oh, no," Sofia started shaking her head. "That's not going to happen."

"Oh, *yes*," he contradicted. "You owe me."

"Come again?"

"Yeah. Just when we got old enough to go hang at the skating rink without chaperones, you dumped me. Remember that?"

"This wouldn't happen to be the same skating rink you took Connie Woods to, would it?"

Ramell's eyebrows raised in surprise. "Oh, so you knew about that, did you?"

"Of course I knew about it." She stiffened and straightened her shoulders. "I also heard that you and Connie were caught necking in the back of the rink next to the boy's bathroom."

He choked.

"Uh-huh. You didn't think I knew about that too, did you?"

"More like I didn't think you cared," he challenged, leaning back in his chair and smiling at her. "Now I just need to figure out if you're just giving me grief or if you're actually jealous."

"Now why would I be jealous of that ten-year-old tramp? For all I know she's probably pulling tricks down on Hollywood Boulevard nowadays."

"She's not pulling tricks. She's a Broadway actress."

Her head jerked toward him. "And how do you know that?"

"She's an A.F.I. client…which I guess now makes her a Limelight client."

Sofia worked her jaw while she reached for her lemonade. "I never knew that. Does she work under her real name?"

Ram laughed. "What? You think I'd tell you now? Look at you?"

"What?"

"My lips are zipped. You're not going to go back into the office and drop her from the company." He laughed.

She shrugged. "I don't know what you're talking about. I was just going to check and see how she was doing…see if she's a good fit for the company."

"Chill out, Sofia. It was just a kiss—a peck, really."

"Uh-huh."

"Actually," he said leaning forward. "I kissed her hoping that the news would get back to you." He reached across the table and picked up her hand.

"Yeah. Likely story," she said, pulling away playfully, but he held firm.

"I have no reason to lie," Ram said. "I had to do something. You refused to talk to me—even at your parents' funeral."

Sofia dropped her gaze and just stared at their connected hands.

"I'm sorry about that," Ram said, quickly wishing he hadn't brought up Sofia's parents.

A silence drifted between them and Sofia could tell that he wanted to pursue his line of questioning and for a few seconds her stomach looped into knots. The last thing that she wanted to do was to ruin their playful mood to start talking about what happened back then. Plus, she still felt uncomfortable at the possibility of having to tell Ramell about his father and her mother—especially since his parents were still married.

"Anyway...Connie and I are just good friends," Ramell said, returning to the subject at hand.

She sensed that he changed the subject for her. Sofia glanced up and met his intense gaze. He was clearly trying to read her like a book. "Don't."

"Don't what?"

"Don't stare. It makes me uncomfortable."

"Then what do you propose I do when I want to let you know that I'm sitting here remembering some of those tricks you showed me this morning?" Ram said, attempting to steer the conversation in yet another direction.

She blushed.

"Do you have any more?" he asked.

It was her turn to lean back and level him with a sultry look. "Maybe."

"Well then, before we get to that, first I think we need to fill in a few blanks."

So much for thinking that she had dodged a bullet. "What sort of blanks?"

"Well, I know a lot about the ten-year-old you, and I definitely know a lot about the—"

"Watch it."

"The *mature businesswoman* side of you, but there a few questions I should know...seeing that we're now man and wife."

"All right. Shoot."

"Okay." He set his beer back down. "Is yellow still your favorite color?"

"It's one of my favorites. I tend to like coral or peach

a little bit more nowadays. How about you? Is blue still your favorite color?"

"Guilty. Favorite song?"

"'Purple Rain.' You?"

"I'm all over the map on that. But if pressed I'm really feeling that joint Charlene and Akil performed at our Pre-Award party."

"'The Journey,'" Sofia said, nodding. "Yeah. I have a feeling that's going to be a big hit for them."

They continued through the standard line of questioning until they eventually reached some stickier topics.

"What was the longest relationship you've ever been in?" Ramell asked.

Sofia shrugged.

"C'mon. You can tell me," he pressed.

"John Davis. We dated when I went to Cambridge. When we were together, I was too busy to notice that he was a complete jerk. Once I graduated and we spent, like, a whole week together, I noticed."

Ram chuckled.

"What about you?" she asked.

"That's easy. I've been in love with one woman my entire life."

Sofia blushed again. "I'm flattered. But we haven't been in a relationship that entire time so come out with it. Who was it and how long?"

He rolled his eyes back and thought about it for a second. "I guess that brings me back to Connie."

"You dated Connie?" she asked incredibly. "I thought you said that it was just a kiss."

"It was just a kiss that night," Ram clarified. "We dated in college for about three months."

"Three months is your longest relationship?"

"Like I said, I've been in love with one woman my entire life. No one else has ever come close, so…"

"So you've had a lifetime of booty calls and one-night stands?"

"Something like that." He started shifting in his chair. "Hey. Don't hate on me because you didn't come around soon enough."

"Look. You're the one that chose this line of questioning."

"Good point. So let's get off this subject before I have to look this John Davis dude up and put him out of his misery."

"Right. And you know Ms. Connie is going to be looking for another agency to represent her when I get back to the office, right?"

Ramell threw back his head and laughed. "Whatever. Come on. We're going skating."

"Uh, wait. I don't know about this," Sofia protested, but Ramell tossed money down on the table and then grabbed her by the hand. Next thing Sofia knew they were renting skates, helmets, knee and elbow pads.

"I'm going to look ridiculous in all of this."

"You're going to look safe," Ram said.

"Then how come you're not wearing all this stuff. I look like a tall three year old."

"Because I know what I'm doing. You haven't been on skates in years."

"More like decades," Sofia clarified.

"Then there you go." He stood up and turned to help her.

Sofia was up for a full minute and then her long legs tried to roll in two different directions. She screamed and then made a desperate lunge for Ramell. He grabbed her and tried to hold her up, but then he toppled over along with her. When they hit the concrete they immediately burst into laughter like pain was funny.

"Well, at least you got busting your butt out of the way pretty quickly." Ram laughed and then helped her back up. "Are you all right?"

Sofia was still laughing so hard that she was crying. "Yeah, I'm fine. I can do this," she affirmed, and then took a deep breath.

"Are you sure?" he asked, helping to wipe away a few tears.

She shook her head no, but said, "Yes."

Thirty minutes later, while she was still a trembling mess on wheels, Ram tried to convince her that she was ready for him to remove his hands.

"No. Don't let go," she begged.

"You're doing fine," he said.

"Wait! Don't!" She started to tremble harder. "Don't do it, Ram," she begged. "I swear I'll never forgive you."

"Is that a fact?" he asked.

"Yes! I'm not trying to break my neck out here."

"You're not going to break your neck."

"How do you know?"

"Because you're already skating by yourself," he

informed her, rolling out to her side so that she could see that she was now skating on her own.

Sofia's eyes nearly bugged out as she glanced down. "I'm skating!"

"I know! Look at you."

Her head jerked toward him as she proclaimed again. "I'm skating by myself!"

"I know!"

"*I'm skating by myself,*" she announced to everyone on the boardwalk.

A few people stared at her but some of them clapped. A big smile exploded across Ram's face at seeing her so happy. Soon they were skating and eating candied apples like a couple of kids. The day breezed by to the point that Sofia was sad to see the sun set. But with Ramell standing next to her and staring at her that sadness was replaced by desire.

"You ready to go home?" he asked.

Home. They had a home together. The whole thing was just so strange to her. It was blowing her mind and stealing her heart at the same time.

"Yeah. Let's go."

Sade's "Soldier of Love" played softly from the speakers that Ramell had set up next to their new bed. After taking a long shower together to wash the day's dirt and grime away, the newlyweds stood in the center of the room, lips locked and smelling like Ivory soap and baby oil. The more their tongues tasted the hungrier they became.

Ramell moaned while his hands made light circles

along Sofia's lower back. His touch was so feathery soft that it caused goosebumps to rise across her body. Her nipples hardened and ached, but they were nothing compared to the iron pipe that was pressing against her brown, wet lips.

Unable to resist, Sofia's slender fingers drifted down between their bodies. She took hold of his oiled rod and started stroking him. Though their mouths were still connected, she felt him gasp. She smiled against his lips. She might not be able to win an argument with him, but she sure as hell held power over him when their clothes came off.

Wielding some of that power, Sofia pulled their lips apart and nibbled her way across his strong jawline until she reached his right ear to whisper, "I want to taste you." She blew a cool stream of air against his lower earlobe. He shivered and then stretched a couple of more inches in her hand. "Oooh. That's a good boy." Slowly her knees dipped until they kissed the floor.

With her head at waist level, Sofia continued to rotate and stroke Ram's thick erection. Just gazing at its smooth length and fat mushroom head made her mouth water. Putting on a timid act, she leaned forward and just swirled her tongue around the tip like it was a piece of candy.

Ramell hissed and stepped forward, hoping that she would open her mouth wide. She didn't accommodate him. Instead, she ran her tongue along the side and then rolled under and slid back up toward the tip. "You're trying to kill me," he panted.

"Now why would I want to do that?"

"I don't know. You must hate me or you wouldn't torture me like this."

"Torture?" Her wonderful tongue moved to the other side. This time inching along at a snail's pace. "I don't know what you're talking about." She glided over a small vein near the top and felt Ram jump reflexively. Sofia smiled and then did it again. Same reaction.

Convinced that she'd found a small G-spot, she concentrated on that area, licking and sucking until Ramell's large hands gently grabbed fistfuls of her hair. Showing no remorse, Sofia stretched her mouth over the head, but made sure her tongue massaged the hell out of that vein.

Ram rolled up onto his toes. Not wanting to come yet, he summoned superhuman strength to jump back and spring himself free from her divine mouth. "You know I'm going to pay you back for that, don't you?"

Sofia put her innocent face on as she blinked up at him. "What did I do?"

"That's not going to work." He took her by her elbows and pulled her up from the floor and before she could process what he was about to do, he lifted one of her legs and pressed it high against his chest so that she had to balance her weight on one leg and lean against him. Ram reached down and squeezed his fat head in between her melting brown sugar and hissed slowly.

Like before, Sofia's mouth sagged open at his initial entry. He was thick, heavy and felt so damn good that a few tears streaked down the corners of her eyes.

With one hand on her stretched leg and the other one

on her hip, Ramell started moving. "How does that feel, baby?"

Sofia couldn't speak and didn't bother to try. She was too busy enjoying all the feelings that he was working out of her body. She was on a fast train to ecstasy and he was definitely driving.

"Uh-huh. I have you now, don't I, baby?" His hips stopped stroking and started pounding. You're not the only one with power in this bedroom, sweetheart." To prove his point, Ram stopped long enough to get a good hold so he could go ahead and lift her completely off the floor and then just bounce her body on top of his length.

It was too much. Sofia could feel her orgasm brewing. When it finally exploded, she threw back her head and released a strangled cry. Ram was right behind her, but with everything rushing to one area, his knees weakened. Finally, his orgasm hit him like a truck and his legs went out from underneath him.

They tumbled to the floor with his body absorbing most of the impact. After the initial shock wore off, they laughed. Like when they fell during skating earlier, once they got started, it was hard to stop.

"I love you so much," Ram said, pulling her close and planting a kiss against the top of her head.

Sofia smiled in the dark, but she was still waiting for that other shoe to drop.

Chapter 16

The next week floated by like a dream. When Sofia and Ram weren't making love, they were trying to patch together plans for their future. When Sofia informed her family about Ramell buying her parents' old home, everyone expressed their joy and excitement for having the house back in the family, especially Rachel. Sofia became obsessed about redecorating and Ram kept dropping hints about them having a real honeymoon.

So caught up with creating their new life together, Sofia started spending less and less time in the office. It didn't mean that she was off her game, she still made and closed some great deals for her clients, but she started spending less time on her BlackBerry and Ram declared their bedroom a no-electronic zone, so the iPad and the laptops had to stay in her new home office.

If there was one thing that was starting to cause Sofia

some anxiety it was the wedding reception her Aunt Lily was planning. It wasn't the list of friends and colleagues that her family invited—it was the fact that Emmett Jordan was going to be there.

Ramell picked up on her apprehension but Sofia struggled with confessing about its source. After all, Emmett was Ram's father and it was clear that the two of them were close. Sofia told herself that she just needed to suck it up. It was just going to be one evening. Surely, she could handle that. If she could glue on fake smiles for Hollywood pow-wow meetings and parties, she could grin and bear being around that lying, backstabbing jerk.

Sofia didn't know how her aunt pulled it off on such short notice, but their wedding reception was booked at the Beverly Wilshire in the heart of Beverly Hills. Both Ramell and Sofia hoped for just a small event with their closest friends and family. Somehow that equaled over a hundred people in her aunt's mind.

Sofia selected a lavender Stella McCartney gown that was all classic chic and timeless on her willowy frame. Her long hair hung in soft, structured waves over her bronze shoulders. When her small team of stylists finished getting her ready and she descended the staircase, Ramell literarily stood at the bottom with his mouth hanging open. Everyone chuckled at his reaction while Sofia simply blushed.

An hour later when they strolled arm and arm into the Beverly Wilshire, the beautiful couple was greeted with an enthusiastic round of applause before being surrounded and congratulated on their marriage. It was at that moment that it truly sunk in for Sofia that she was indeed a married woman. The idea was both scary and thrilling at the same time.

Uncle Jacob and Aunt Lily swept their way over and showered Ram and Sofia with hugs and kisses.

"I'm just so happy for the two of you," Lily said, blotting away her tears before they had a chance to ruin her makeup. "You're both just so beautiful together. I know in my heart of hearts that you two were destined to be together."

Ramell's arm draped around Sofia's slim waist and then pulled her closer. "That's what I keep telling her." He smiled at her and couldn't resist leaning in for a quick kiss.

A few minutes later, Rachel and her fiancé Ethan Chambers approached. With their own wedding a week away, the happy couple glowed with love.

"It looks like we're going to be brothers soon," Ethan said to Ramell, thrusting out his hand.

"I'm looking forward to it," Ramell said, pumping his hand. "But I'm also expecting you to take good care of Rachel here. If not, I would hate to have to hunt you down."

"That would make two of us," Uncle Jacob cut in.

Ethan pulled at his collar to let them know that he could feel the invisible noose they were threatening him with. "I don't think that you guys have anything to worry about." He pulled Rachel close and captured her with a kiss.

Ramell frowned and then glanced over at Sofia. "I think we can do better than that, don't you?"

Sofia smiled. "I don't know. Do you think?"

Ramell straightened his arm and then in dramatic form grabbed Sofia, dipped her back so that she kicked one foot up and then laid a kiss on her that was reminiscent of the old black-and-white classic movies. When he finally lifted her back up, the entire room erupted into applause.

Ethan and Rachel laughed at their antics.

"Since this is your reception. I'm going to let you win this round," Ethan joked.

Ramell winked. "Smart man."

Emmett Jordan's voice boomed as he approached. "Hello, son!"

Instantly, Sofia stiffened. Her gaze shifted to Rachel who, with one glance, telepathed silent support.

"So you finally did it!" he laughed, whacking his son on the back. "You finally married her. I have to admit I was beginning to have my doubts. Then again, women can't resist the Jordan charm."

Ramell laughed as he returned his father's hug. "I'm glad you could make it, pop."

"I wouldn't have missed it for the world. Well, I did miss the wedding," he reminded him.

"Sorry about that, pop." Ram tightened his hold around Sofia's waist. "It was sort of a spontaneous thing."

"Is that right?" Emmett's gaze finally drifted over to his new daughter-in-law. "My God. You look so much like your mother," he said, shaking his head.

Sofia was already on a low simmer and her smile was starting to wilt.

"How about a hug?" he asked, stretching his arm wide.

She'd rather gouge her own eyes out with a pitchfork, but it was time for the big Hollywood agent to put the acting chops she'd learned to work. After making Emmett wait for a couple of awkward seconds, she finally stepped into his embrace. However, she didn't allow for his arms to stay around her for long as she quickly removed herself from his embrace. She caught Ramell's frown from the corner of her eyes, but she refused to look at him. Instead, she forced her lips to curl back up so that she could ask to be excused.

"I just need to dip into the ladies' room for a second," Sofia said, stepping away from Ramell's side.

"I'll come with you," Rachel offered. She gave her fiancé a brief kiss and then peeled herself out of his arms.

The two sisters rushed from the small circle just shy of leaving skid marks. Seeing their speed most of their guests started parting like the Red Sea to avoid being run over. Sofia couldn't get away fast enough and could barely manage to fill her collapsing lungs with much needed oxygen as she reached the ladies' room.

"Are you all right?" Rachel asked.

"I will be," Sofia said, pulling in several more deep breaths. "I swear I can't stand that man!"

"I know," Rachel said, rubbing her back in hopes of calming her down. "It's just for one evening. You can do this."

"And after tonight?" Sofia challenged. "What if he's around all the time? What if Ram invites him over to dinner once or twice a week? What if they get together and hang out in the media room for football and basketball games?" Heat rushed up her chest and neck as she worked herself up into a frenzy. When she started feeling lightheaded and woozy, she grabbed a hold of the vanity to support herself.

"Calm down, Sofia. Calm down," Rachel urged. "Deep breaths. Take deep breaths."

After feeling the tips of her ears burning, Sofia took her sister's suggestion and started taking in deep breaths and expelling them slowly.

"That's it. Calm down," Rachel coached. "You can do it."

Bit by bit, Sofia's face cooled as she calmed down.

Rachel smiled. "There you go. Do you feel better?"

Sofia nodded and then hugged her sister. "Yes. Thank you. I really appreciate it."

"You know I'm always here for you." Her sister smiled. "But as far as dealing with your new father-in-law, I think you're just going to have to talk to Ramell and tell him how you feel about Emmett."

"Yeah. I should really tell my new husband that I can't stand his father. That should go over well."

"There's something to be said for honesty. You can't go the rest of your lives together trying to avoid the man. Ram is going to understand—he might even be able to help you two work this thing out."

Sofia stiffened. "I do not want to work anything out with that man."

Rachel tossed her hands up. "I understand. But you're going to have to talk to Ramell about the situation regardless. There's no getting around that."

She hesitated, but after her sister cocked her head and

stretched her eyebrows up at her, Sofia had to admit that she was right. "I'll do it tonight."

"Good," Rachel said, giving her another hug. "Now are you ready to go back out there?"

She sucked in one more deep breath and then nodded.

"All right. Let's go get them, tiger." Rachel draped her arm around her older sister's shoulders and then led her out of the ladies' room.

They hadn't taken more than a couple of steps outside the door before Emmett Jordan cornered them.

"Sofia, do you think that I can talk to you for a few minutes?"

Sofia dropped all pretense of a smile. "I don't think that now is a good time," she said coldly. But when she attempted to step around him, he blocked her and Rachel's path. "It will only take a minute."

"Then call my office and make an appointment."

Emmett shook his head. "My God. You really do hate me," he said, frowning and shaking his head. "I think I've always suspected it since you had walked in on—"

"I don't want to talk about this right now!" Sofia yelled as she tried to move around him again, only for Emmett to pull the same stunt and block off her exit.

"Wait!"

"Will you stop doing that?" Sofia snapped and stomped her foot.

When a few heads swiveled in their direction, Rachel leaned over and whispered, "Take a deep breath. It's going to be all right."

Sofia followed her sister's instructions. "Look, Emmett. This isn't the time or the place for this."

"I just want to clear the air. I think that there's a huge misunderstanding that's gone on for far too long. And now that…well, we're family…"

Sofia stiffened again. Why couldn't this man get it through his head that she didn't want to talk to him?

"…And family is important to me…" he continued as he stepped into her personal space.

Alarm bells rang in her head as she quickly jumped back and held up her hands like stop signs. "Emmett, we're not about to have this conversation."

Rachel stepped forward. "Mr. Jordan, maybe this isn't such a good time."

"Is there a problem over here?" Ramell asked, threading his way into the circle.

"There's no problem," Sofia lied.

"I think there's a big problem," Emmett contradicted.

Ram frowned.

"What's going on?" Uncle Jacob and Aunt Lily now joined the loop.

Sofia's blood pressure shot up as she placed her slim fingers against her temples.

"I was just trying to talk to Sofia about a few things," Emmett pressed.

"And I said that I didn't want to talk right now," Sofia hissed. "I don't want to talk to you *ever*. Period. End of story."

"Sofia," Ram said, stunned. "What's gotten into you,

sweetheart?" He moved closer to her and wrapped his arm back around her for support.

"Nothing has gotten into me. Will you just drop it?" She tried to pull away, but he wouldn't have it. "Will you let me go? Stop trying to control me!"

"What?" Ramell's arm fell away from her waist.

"Maybe we just need to go into another room real quick so that we can talk," Uncle Jacob suggested. "Clearly, we do need to clear the air about a few things."

What had gotten into everyone? Didn't they just hear her say that she didn't want to talk to this man?

"I don't know," Rachel hedged. "Sofia is getting pretty upset. Maybe we should do this another time."

"Well, I, for one, want to know what the hell is going on," Ram said, his gaze still searching his wife's face for the harsh rebuke that she'd just lashed out on him.

Sofia wanted to apologize, but at the same time she felt as if she was being cornered. And now that her family was all looking like she was the freak in a freak show, she relented so that she could just get this whole thing over with. "Fine." She tossed up her hands. "Five minutes."

Emmett had the audacity to smile now that he'd gotten his way.

"Let's just go into this room over here," Uncle Jacob said, pointing off to the side.

Unbelievably, in the middle of their own wedding reception, the family smiled and excused themselves to their few friends and family so that they could dip into a room off from the grand room.

Ram took a chance and swung his arm back around

her waist. She allowed it, but she was still irritated. This was the very thing that she had hoped to avoid for years, now it was worse than she had ever imagined it. Instead of privately telling Ram her issues about his father, she now how to air her grievances in front of her whole family. Once they were all piled into the other room, Uncle Jacob closed the door.

"First of all," Jacob began, turning toward Sofia. "I'm sorry that we have to do this this evening, but clearly it's time that we deal with a few things, a few things that… your aunt and I had hoped to avoid." He reached over for his wife's hand.

Sofia folded her arms. "My problem isn't with you or Aunt Lily. This is about Emmett and him alone," she stressed. "It's about how *he* stabbed my father in the back. It's about *him* sneaking around with my mother!"

"*What?*" Ram thundered, turning toward his father.

Emmett's hands came up as he stepped back. "That is not true!"

"Yes it is," Sofia contradicted him. "I was there, remember?"

"What? You saw them together or something?" Ram asked.

"No." Sofia shook her head. "I was there that day my father called him out on it." Her gaze swung back to Emmett. "You remember that?"

Emmett lowered his hands as sadness crept over his face. "Of course I remember that day. But you got it wrong, Sofia. Just like your father got it wrong. And in the end he didn't believe any of that nonsense. He was just lashing out."

"No." Sofia shook her head. "He called you out for the lying backstabber that you are!"

"Sofia," Aunt Lily gasped.

"It's true, Aunt Lily. Come on. You were there, too." Ram's head swiveled to his father. "Dad, is it true?"

"No," Emmett said simply.

Uncle Jacob stepped forward. "He's telling the truth, Sofia. You were too young at the time to understand what was going on. For a long time I thought that you'd forgotten about that day. Heck, I have sometimes forgotten that you had walked in there that day. Given that the accident was just a couple of days later, we—your aunt and I—just concentrated on being there for you and your sister. And part of being there for you was also trying to shield something from both you and the crazy media attention we generated at the time. I knew that you were angry, but I didn't understand the depth of this until the A.F.I. merger."

Sofia tried to keep up with the conversation, but none of it was making any sense yet.

Jacob drew a deep breath. "What you walked in on that day…was an intervention."

"A what?" Sofia frowned.

"An intervention for your father," he said, moving closer. "There's no easy way to say this, girls, but your father had a drinking problem."

Sofia started shaking her head. *This was all a big lie.*

"We had all gathered there that day to confront him. At first I didn't think anything of it. And I was his twin. I always thought that I knew everything about him. We've always had such a strong connection. You know that. We were best friends our entire lives. People used to label him the fun one and I was the serious one of the two. Then one day the cracks started to show and then there started to be too many to hide. He started losing money and the business we had poured all our blood, sweat and tears into was threatened. He was gambling, taking out loans I didn't know about. The next thing I know we were surrounded by creditors.

"Your mother, Lily, tried several times to convince him to go to AA, but your father wouldn't hear of it. He didn't think that he had a problem. When it was clear to all of us, except to John, that Limelight was teetering on the edge of bankruptcy, *I* approached Emmett about a possible merger. When John found out he became convinced that Emmett was trying to steal the company from him. Unfortunately, he found out the same evening that we had staged the intervention. And he came in drunk and belligerent. He said a whole lot of stuff that he didn't mean."

Sofia kept shaking her head. "My father wasn't a drunk. How can you say that?"

Aunt Lily stepped forward. "Sofia, I know all of this is a big shock, but what you heard—"

"What I heard was not the truth!" She pushed back out of Ram's arms. "I remember my father and he was not a drunk. He was loving and caring—"

"Yes," Uncle Jacob said. "He was all those things— but he had a problem." He drew a deep breath. "Which is why he finally agreed to go to rehab…in Colorado."

Both Sofia and Rachel gasped.

Jacob nodded. "*That* was where he and your mother were going when their plane crashed. He was going to get help."

Aunt Lily wiped tears from her eyes. "There hasn't been a day that any of us hasn't wrestled with the cruel irony that the only reason that they were even on that plane was to try to save his life. I know how much you love and cherish the memory of your father, Sofia. That had a lot to do with our decision to not tell you about his problem. And it isn't fair to Emmett for you to believe those wild accusations your father tossed at him. They weren't true and he doesn't deserve it."

"No." Sofia continued shaking her head. "It's not true. It's not. My father was a good man. He was a hard worker and…"

"Yes, yes, and yes," Lily said. "But he was still just a man. A man that needed help."

Tears started pouring down Sofia's face and she couldn't stop shaking her head. "Why would you? How could you?" She placed a hand over her mouth.

"Baby." Ram reached for her but she jumped out of his grasp.

"Don't touch me," she snapped and then tried to suck in a deep breath. Instead she started hyperventilating. "Don't ever touch me." Her gaze zoomed back to her aunt and uncle and she wanted to lash out at them too, but couldn't get the mean words off her tongue.

Rachel rushed to her side. "Sofia, honey. You're turning red. Try to calm down."

"How can I calm down when they're saying…" She shook her head. "I don't believe it. I refuse to believe it.

My father was not a drunk. He was a good man and I'm not about to just stand here while you all drag his name and his memory through the mud! I won't! I—" Just then the room started spinning and there didn't seem to be enough oxygen for Sofia to breathe.

Ram rushed forward to his wife just as she started to sink toward the floor. "Sofia!"

Chapter 17

Ramell didn't wait for the paramedics to be called. Once Sofia collapsed, he spent a full minute trying to wake her up. When she wouldn't wake he swept her into his arms and raced out of the room. *"Please get out of the way."*

A collective gasp rose above the glittering Hollywood elite while they quickly jumped out of the way. The Wellesleys and Ethan Chambers all raced right behind him as Ram jetted out of the Wilshire. Less than twenty minutes later, they all piled into Cedars-Sinai Hospital Emergency Room. Upon seeing an unconscious woman draped in his arms, doctors and nurses rushed toward him and then pried her out of his arms.

"What happened?" A young man, dressed in a pair of blue scrubs, who looked like he was barely old enough to have a driver's license, started checking Sofia over.

"I'm not quite sure. She just fainted," Ram said and then a memory flashed. "It might have something to do with her blood pressure. I know that she's taking something for it."

The young man nodded, placed her on a rolling gurney and then pushed Sofia's eyelids open.

"Is she going to be all right?" Ram asked, hovering over the doctor's shoulders.

"She's going to be fine, sir," the man said, plugging his ears with his stethoscope and then checking Sofia's heartbeat.

Everyone was rushing around at warp speed, but Ram made sure that he stayed on top of everything that was going on. It was difficult because every time he looked down at Sofia lying on the gurney, she looked so small and vulnerable that it was causing a tight restriction in his chest and his eyes to feel as if someone had poured battery acid in them. He didn't like seeing his wife like this and he was angry about his part in getting her so upset. She had made it very clear that she didn't want to talk to his father and they had all insisted that they try to clear the air about her father's past.

It was a lot of startling information about a man she had spent her entire life idolizing. Ramell had known about Limelight's near bankruptcy once upon a time, but his father certainly never told him that it was because John Wellesley had a gambling and alcohol problem. Maybe because his father always knew about his feelings toward Sofia and possibly feared he would tell her about it. Apparently they had all agreed to bury John's demons in order to protect his children.

The media coverage was intense when John and Vivian passed, but the paparazzi back then was a different animal and not every rock was overturned on their personal life. If it had been, surely John's problems would have been splashed everywhere. Instead the coverage just focused on the tragedy and the fate of the children. Now he wished he would've known. Knowing now that she had walked into that intense intervention and misunderstood all that she heard, it made sense why she fought their companies' merger as hard as she did.

Now he finally understood why she had ended their friendship. All those years he thought it was because of something he had done.

Twenty minutes later, Sofia was wheeled into a private room and their entire clan followed closed behind. Not long after that, Sofia moaned and her eyelashes started fluttering.

"She's waking up," Lily said, clutching her left hand.

Ram held her right one. When Sofia opened her beautiful brown eyes he was finally able to pull in his first full breath and offer up a prayer of gratitude. He lifted her hand and brushed a kiss against the back of it before smiling and speaking softly, "Hey, baby. You gave us quite a scare. How are you feeling?"

Their eyes locked and a string of pear-shaped tears slid down the side of her face. But instead of answering, she pulled her hand free from his and then turned away from him.

His smile melted as confusion and disbelief crashed in on his hopeful expression.

Lily swept Sofia's hair from her face while Rachel and Jacob crowded around the bed. "The doctor says that you're going to be all right," Lily informed her. "Your blood pressure was elevated pretty high and...well, baby. We're so sorry. We didn't mean to upset you so badly. We just—"

"I don't want to talk about it," Sofia croaked, but then started coughing.

Ram turned toward the small table next to the bed and quickly poured her a small plastic cup of water and then offered it to her.

Still coughing, she hesitated for a moment, but then gave in and accepted it, along with his help, when he pressed it up against her lips. She started off with small sips, but then ended up gulping it down. He poured her another cup, but she waved it away.

"Feeling any better?" Rachel asked.

Sofia nodded, but there was still tears rolling down her face. After a minute, she spoke. "I appreciate you all being here, but I need some time alone."

Everyone opened their mouths to say something, but she cut them off cold. "Please."

Their gazes shifted among themselves, but this time they were determined to respect her wishes. "All right," Ram said. "We can all just step outside, if you like."

She shook her head. "No. You don't understand. I don't want you all to wait outside. I need time...without any hovering."

Her words were like steel bullets through his heart. "Sofia, I think we need to talk."

She swallowed, but still refused to look at him. "And we will. Just not right now."

No one moved.

"Please," she begged again. She closed her eyes but her tears soaked through her long lashes.

Struggling to understand, Ramell lowered his head and brushed a kiss against her turned cheek. In that moment, he knew that his marriage was in trouble. He pulled away from her while the pain in his heart nearly became unbearable, but he released her hand and backed away.

Jacob, Lily, Rachel and Ethan also started drifting away from the bed and then they all marched toward the door with their heads hung low. But before they all ushered out, Sofia spoke, "Rachel...you can stay."

Rachel gave them a sympathetic look but turned back and rushed to her sister's side. The rest of them were clearly dismissed. Heart broken, pride shattered, Ram left the hospital with his own tears streaming down his face.

Chapter 18

Sofia left the hospital with a new prescription and a doctor's warning for her to manage her stress better—which she answered by throwing herself head long back into work. However, this time she refused to step one foot into Limelight Entertainment. She returned to her penthouse and worked out of her home office. She didn't want to see her aunt and uncle or even Ramell and Emmett. She couldn't. Just like she couldn't wrap her brain around the man they portrayed her father to be.

Every time she closed her eyes, all she could remember was the father that would take time to play tea or dress up with her—even when he was tired. She would remember the times he would read her bedtime stories and fill her head with fantasies about princes and princesses. Her father was everything to her. Everything.

He was kind, handsome and strong. Even now she

remembered how she used to feel like she was on top of the world whenever she would ride on his shoulders. And so many people loved him. They used to have parties at their house all the time. She remembered sneaking down to see all the Hollywood stars of the time in their beautiful clothes—laughing, smiling…and drinking.

Sofia snapped out of her reverie in time to hear an offer from a studio executive buzzing in her ear. "What kind of deal are we talking about?" she asked, standing up from her office chair and waltzing over to the window to stare out at the cityscape. "I don't know. That sounds awfully low," she said, even though she wasn't listening to what Frasier was offering. It didn't matter. Her job was to play hardball.

That was pretty much her routine for the next few days—that and screening her calls.

What Sofia was going through wasn't Ramell's fault. It wasn't even her aunt and uncle's fault. It was the foundation of who and what she believed crumbling beneath her that made her question everything—especially everything that had happened in the past month. Work didn't comfort her, but it kept her busy. And being busy kept her from breaking down.

But just barely.

However, the more she linked back into her own routine, the more she started distancing herself from the decisions she'd made in the past month. Getting married in Las Vegas the way she did. How cliché could they get? Hardly anything she'd done since Ramell merged his way into her life was like her. Making out in public places, dancing on tables and drinking and blacking out—who was that girl?

Much later that night, Sofia attended a small viewing party for a new movie from a popular director. She smiled. She laughed. She went through the motions. But her heart just wasn't into her performance.

She just wanted to make an appearance and then head back to her place, but as luck would have it, her uncle was also attending the party.

"You've been avoiding me," Jacob said.

Sofia sucked in a deep breath. She wasn't ready for this. "I know. I'm sorry."

"I know this isn't the place, but I really wish that we could sit down and talk. Maybe after your sister's wedding tomorrow. Your aunt and I would *really* like to talk to you about why we kept certain things from you."

"I know why. I just…can't get myself to believe it. And I can't believe I had everything so wrong for so long. I'm just trying to adjust." Sofia shrugged. "It's going to take some time."

He nodded as if he understood. "Still. Your aunt would like to hear from you. She's blaming herself for a lot stuff right now and I don't think that's fair. Everything we did we did out of love. We may not have always gotten it right, but no one is perfect."

"I know that."

"Do you?"

Sofia frowned and then finally recognized the look on her uncle's face as disappointment. That wasn't something that she was used to seeing from him.

"I'm just going to say this and then I'm going to let it go. I loved my brother. Being twins, we shared a strong bond. There was nothing I wouldn't do for him and I know that he felt the same way about me. He was a good man. And just because he struggled with an illness didn't make him any less of a man. In the end he recognized that and he was going to get help. He did it for me, for your mother, and most of all he did it for you and your sister. John loved both of you so much that he wanted to be the best father he could be. And nothing we told you the other day should change how you feel about him, how you've always felt about him."

Jacob's words of wisdom caused a tear to skip down her face. She quickly brushed a finger beneath her eyes and sniffed. "You're right," she admitted. It all suddenly became crystal clear to her. There was no point in trying to fit a square block into a round hole. People were complicated and they had many different sides to them.

"We'll talk after the wedding tomorrow," her uncle said, even though it sounded like a question.

"I'd like that." She leaned forward and brushed a kiss against his cheek. "And I'll call Aunt Lily tonight."

"Thanks. She'd love that."

"I was hoping I would run into you here."

Sofia stiffened with her drink pressed against her lips when she recognized the voice behind her. Her heart hammering, she slowly turned around and met her husband's tense and probing stare.

Uncle Jacob cut in, "I'll just leave you two alone." He stepped back then turned and drifted into the crowd.

"You look good." Ram's gaze roamed over her simple blue dress. "I hope that's not alcohol. It doesn't mix well with your medication, you know. And I don't want you running off and marrying someone else."

"Ramell," she whispered.

"Ah. So you do remember me. I was worried there for a moment since you haven't returned any of my calls." He smiled but it didn't reach his eyes.

"I was going to call."

"Good to know."

"I just needed some time." She glanced around to make sure that they weren't drawing too much attention.

"Time for what?" he challenged, sliding a hand into his pocket. Somehow he managed to look aloof and pissed off at the same time.

"To think," she answered, lowering her voice further. "I just got hit with a lot, you know, all at once."

He bobbed his head. "Yeah. I believe I was there. You know this is generally the time when a couple tries to come together. If you're hurting then I hurt." Slowly his smile melted. "But what *kills* me is that after all these years you still don't come to me. Not when we were best friends and not when we're man and wife."

"Ram—"

"No. Let me finish." He cleared his throat and lifted his chin. "You have a habit of just putting me on a shelf and then going on about your life. And like a fool I just let you do it."

Sofia frowned as cracks in Ramell's controlled expression started to show. "That's not…that's not what I'm doing."

"Don't insult me, Sofia. Every night I go to *our* house, hoping that you'll be there. And you're not. You've gone back to your penthouse, back to your beloved job, and back to ignoring me and my calls."

Fear clutched Sofia's heart. Seeing the sincerity in Ram's eyes forced her to let her guard down and she could finally see herself through his eyes and she could feel what he was feeling right now. She stepped forward and reached for his hand, but he stepped back.

"You don't have to say anything. I'm going to make this easy for you, Sofia. I'll file for an annulment. Clearly this whole marriage thing was a mistake."

"No, Ram. That's not it at all."

He shook his head. "That is it. Look. I'm going to be honest with you, Sofia. I love you. I always have and I always will. But I can't continue to do this with you. I can't keep waiting for you to love me as much as I love you. I just can't. I'll talk to Jacob. I can transfer to work out of our New York office. That should make things easier and we won't have to worry about running into each other at the office."

"Ramell, that's not necessary."

"For me it is. It will just make all of this a lot easier, for the both of us."

He stepped forward and then planted a kiss on her forehead.

"Goodbye, Sofia."

Chapter 19

The next morning, Sofia woke with red, swollen eyes. She had spent the whole night staring at the phone and drenching her pillow with tears. The few times that she managed to drift off to sleep her mind would replay the scene of Ramell telling her that he was going to file for an annulment. Each time it repeated she would experience the same stabbing pain in her heart. But what had she expected? She was guilty of everything that he'd accused her of. She cut him off when they were children over some stupid misunderstanding and then she did the same thing again these past few days. And because of what? Because she couldn't handle hearing that her father wasn't perfect?

Ramell was right. Why didn't she turn to him in her time of trouble and not away from him? It wasn't like she didn't trust him. She did. She trusted him with her life. Climbing out of bed, Sofia shuffled to the bathroom to see how bad the damage was. It was worse than she thought. Bed head, red eyes, puffy nose—she looked like a train wreck and she had to be on a plane to Napa Valley in a couple of hours.

She headed for the shower even though all she really wanted to do was go back and climb into bed. But there was no peace there, either. Her thoughts tortured her as she scrubbed and rinsed. *I can't keep waiting for you to love me as much as I love you.* Sofia's tears blended with the hot water spraying down from the showerhead. By the time she turned off the water she was rubbed raw and her fingertips looked pickled.

Realizing that she needed to hurry, Sofia attempted to pick up the pace, but she was sluggish at best. When she got into her car, she had every intention of going straight to the airport but the minute she hit the highway she drove to her old house instead. "Please be here. Please be here," she prayed feverishly. In the driveway, she'd barely put the car in Park before hopping out and running into the house.

"Ramell," Sofia shouted as she jetted through the house. She kept calling out for him as she ran from room to room. He wasn't there. When she reached their bedroom, she was shocked to discover that his clothes weren't there. Not in the walk-in closets, not in the drawers—not anywhere.

"Oh my God. What have I done?" Sofia slapped a hand against her mouth while a fresh wave of acid tears started to burn the back of her eyes. She needed to fix this. But how?

Think. Think. She fixed problems all the time. Being a good agent meant being a problem solver. *I don't think I can solve this one.* Sofia walked over to the bed and sat down for a few minutes. In the back of her mind, she knew that she needed to get over to the airport. Her sister was getting married that afternoon, but the other part of her wanted—no—needed, to find her own husband. She needed to stop him from filing an annulment.

Torn, she hopped up from the bed and returned to her car. While she drove out to the highway, she picked up her cell phone, took a deep breath and called Ramell. Hopefully, he wasn't too mad at her that he wouldn't answer his phone. At least that was her prayer…until her call went to voicemail. She was about to hang up but then waited too long and heard the beep. "Uh, hello, Ram. It's me. Sofia." She cleared her throat. "Look, I've been thinking a lot about what you said last night. You know the whole thing about you thinking our getting married being a mistake and you, well you know—"

Beep!

"Damn it." Sofia tossed her phone over to the passenger seat and then slapped a hand against the steering wheel in frustration. Heartbroken, she made it over to the private airport. She was twenty minutes late, but her uncle held the private jet until she got there. She quickly apologized for her tardiness and climbed aboard.

Actually, she had a lot of apologies to make, she realized upon boarding the plane, the first one being with her Aunt Lily.

"Don't worry about it, baby," her aunt said, cupping her face. "All that matters is that you're all right."

Sofia wasn't all right, but she had worried them enough. Plus, it was supposed to be a happy day. Rachel's day. She was going to put a smile on her face and be there for her little sister. When the plane took off, Sofia glanced out the window and stared out at the white fluffy clouds. Ram said that all his troubles faded when he was in the sky. She waited for that feeling to come over her now. But there was nothing on earth that was going to make her feel better about losing the best thing that had ever happened to her.

Nothing.

The beauty of Napa Valley rolled past Sofia without her noticing. She sat in the car next to her aunt with her thoughts tumbling over the mess that she made with Ramell. Beside her, Aunt Lily exclaimed at the vineyards they passed while riding up to the Chambers Winery.

"This is such a wonderful place for a wedding." Lily clasped her hands together. "I know I'm going to cry."

Jacob chuckled. "You always cry at weddings."

"True. But today there's going to be some real water-works."

"Don't worry about it. I come bearing handkerchiefs." He wrapped his arm around his wife and delivered a quick kiss against her temple. He noticed his other niece brooding on the other side of the car, but held his tongue. When they arrived at the Chambers' breathtaking château, he helped his wife out of the car and then lingered to offer a hand to Sofia. He already suspected what was going on but he asked anyway. "Everything all right, Sofia?"

She instantly plastered on a fake smile. "Fine. I'm doing just…" she met his knowing eyes and came clean. "I messed up," she admitted. "I messed up badly."

Jacob pulled in a deep breath and slid an arm around her waist. "Is there anything I can help you with?"

"I wish that you could, but…I don't think anything can fix this."

He cocked his head. "It's not like you to just give up."

"I know, but—"

"Then don't start making it a habit now." He squeezed her waist as they headed toward the front door.

Sofia let her uncle's words hang in her head. The more she thought about it, the more she drew strength from them. They were quickly introduced to Ethan's parents as well as his older brother, Hunter, and his six-year-old niece Kendra. They were a beautiful family that was clearly a close-knit unit. And when Livia Blake entered the room and slid an arm around Hunter, Sofia felt a kick. It wasn't jealousy this time, but longing.

Excited, Lily clasped her hands together. "Well, I hope everyone is ready for a fantastic wedding,"

The women said their goodbyes to the men and headed off to a separate wing of the house that was temporarily dubbed the bridal suite. Rachel, who was sitting in a chair with a hairstylist, jumped from her chair, screaming, *"Guess who's getting married today!"*

"You are," the women screamed back and then rushed forward for a group hug. Music, champagne, hor d'oeuvres, before long there was a full party in swing. Sofia's mood lightened. She loved seeing her baby sister

so happy. Rachel positively glowed while she recounted the story of how she and Ethan met and fell in love on the set of *Paging the Doctor.*

"Well it's not like I'm the only one getting married." Rachel turned toward Charlene and then all the ladies in the room followed suit.

Charlene cradled her hands on her thick waist. "I wasn't going to say anything. It's your day."

Rachel waved that comment off and reached for her girl's hand and thrust it toward the other women. "Bam! Look at that sucker."

All the women blinked at the mammoth rock that Akil had put on her finger.

Sofia's mouth hung open just like the rest of them and she wondered how she hadn't noticed the ring when she first saw her. It was just that big. "That *definitely* says that you're off the market," Sofia said and all the women laughed.

"And what about you, Livia?" Charlene asked. "Have any news that you'd like to share with us ladies?"

You've got to be kidding me. Sofia turned her head toward Livia, who was now blushing as hard as Charlene.

"What? You want me to talk about this? *Bam!*" She thrust out her hand, also adorned with a beautiful, equally sizable diamond.

"And?" Rachel prodded.

"And…Hunter and I should be hearing the pitter-patter of little crawling feet by summer."

There was a collective, "Oh my God," before every one rushed to hug and congratulate Livia. At least now

Sofia knew the real reason why Livia had recently quit the business.

"And let's not forget my big sister, Sofia," Rachel chimed.

Sofia shook her head. She definitely didn't want the attention on her.

"She recently got married, too," Rachel continued.

Sofia hadn't gotten around to telling Rachel that Ram was filing for an annulment. And she certainly wasn't about to tell her right now, either.

"Let's see the ring," one of her sister's friends said.

Sofia glanced down at the simple band that she and Ram picked out during their quickie marriage and couldn't help but smile when she thrust it forward. "I believe that it was the best one Elvis had in his display counter," she chuckled.

"Well I can testify that it was certainly an interesting ceremony," Charlene said. "And after taking a peek at that video clip floating around, at least Akil and I now know why Ramell wasn't wearing a shirt when we showed up."

Sofia slapped a hand across her face while the women laughed. "So much for what happens in Vegas stays in Vegas."

Luckily Sofia was soon spared any further inquiry about her marriage and she went back to just celebrating Rachel's day.

"Oh I wonder if Uncle Jacob remembered to write his toast," Rachel said. "The last time I talked to him he said that he hadn't gotten around to it."

"I'm sure he has," Sofia reassured her.

"I don't know. Uncle Jacob likes to adlib a lot, and he's not as good at it as he thinks he is."

The girls laughed. "Sofia, can you call him and check?"

Sofia grabbed her purse, but then remembered that she had left her cell phone in the passenger seat of her car. "I'm sorry but I don't have my cell phone with me."

Instantly, everyone stopped what they were doing and gawked at Sofia.

"What?"

"All right. Hold up. Who are you and what have you done with my sister?" Rachel asked with her hands on her hips.

Sofia frowned at all their stunned expressions. "What do you mean?"

"You never forget your phone," Rachel told her. "Never."

Sofia thought about it. Lately she hadn't been as much of a slave to her gadgets as she used to be and…it felt good. "Hollywood can wait… every once in a while," she said with a wink.

Everyone applauded.

After makeup, manicures, and intricate hairstyles, the women all shimmied into their dresses in time for the wedding photographer to usher them to a designated area and take the first round of pictures. Rachel looked like an angel floating around in her white dress and striking poses.

When the women finished taking their pictures, they headed back toward the bridal suite. Bringing up the rear, Sofia and Charlene were laughing as Livia told them adorable stories of her soon-to-be stepdaughter. It was clear to everyone that she was going to make a wonderful mother. They turned down the wrong corner and ran directly into the groom and the groomsmen.

"Afternoon, ladies," Ethan greeted.

Sofia sucked in a startled breath when her eyes zeroed in on Ramell.

"Ooops. I guess we should have taken that left turn at Albuquerque," Livia laughed. "But first," she rushed over to Hunter, "let me just steal a quick kiss."

The small group laughed…all except for Sofia and Ramell, who were both left standing off to the side. "What are you doing here?" she finally asked.

Ram cleared his throat and forced on a smile. "I, uh—"

"I invited him," Ethan said. "After all, in about an hour he's going to be my new brother-in-law." He gave Ramell a good, hearty whack on the back. "Besides, I had a cousin that had to back out at the last minute and it just all worked out."

Sofia swallowed. There were a million things going through her mind at the moment and she couldn't settle on a single one to say. Their laughter died down and an uncomfortable silence started to hug the group.

"Well, we're just going to head on back to the blushing bride," Charlene said, tugging on Livia's arm.

"Yeah. We don't want them to think something happened to us."

"Can I come with?" Ethan joked.

"No." Charlene waved a finger at him. "It's bad luck to see the bride before the wedding."

Ethan tossed up his hands. "Fine. I guess we'll just go get our pictures taken."

The bridesmaids and the groomsmen started to part ways. Sofia's moment was about to pass her by. *Stop him! Stop him!*

"Ramell, can I talk to you for a moment?" she said so quickly that it sounded like one long word.

Ram stopped in his tracks and turned back to face her.

"Please?" She glanced at the others and then tried to swallow the large lump in the center of her throat. "It'll just take a moment."

No one waited for a brick to fall onto their head. They quickly scrambled out of the hallway. Sofia hesitated because she had the distinct impression that Ram wanted to leave, as well. Was it too late?

"I…" She stopped, feeling her throat closing up on her. She closed her eyes at the threat of tears. "I've never been at a lost for words," she said and tried to laugh at herself, but even that fell flat.

"Maybe that's a sign, too," Ram said.

Eyes shimmering, she looked up to see tears shining in his eyes.

"Love isn't supposed to be this hard," he said.

Sofia shook her head. "I think you're wrong about that. If it wasn't hard then everyone would have it. Love is hard to find. Love is hard to wait for. And in my case it was hard to recognize. And even harder to appreciate." She sniffed and then backhanded a few tears. "I'm…I'm sorry. I'm just so damn sorry about how I've treated you. You were right about everything you said last night.

You've always been there for me, even when I convinced myself that I didn't want you to be. I took you for granted and there's nothing…nothing I can say can ever excuse that."

Ramell nodded and lowered his gaze.

"But you never had to wait for me to love you. I've always loved you. And if you give me another chance, I promise to prove it to you every day for the rest of our lives. I don't want you to move to New York and I don't want an annulment."

"Sofia—"

"No. Please let me finish." She reached for his hand and then took comfort with the fact that he didn't snatch it back from her. "You mean more to me than even I knew at first. It wasn't until I was faced with the possibility of really losing you that I realized just how much you're a part of me. I love kissing you, making love to you. Hell, I even love fighting with you. But I can't…I absolutely can't imagine myself going back to living without you. Not this time." She took a timid step forward and slid her hands flat against his chest. "Please. Give me a chance to love you the way that you deserve to be loved. I'll work less hours. I promise that I'll never put you on a shelf again. I'll—"

"Sofia—"

"Don't say it's too late." Tears streamed down her face. "I don't know what I'll do if you say that it's too late." She searched his eyes for any sign that he still loved her, that he still wanted her.

Ramell lifted her hands from his chest and brought

them up to his lips. In that moment she feared that this was it. Her second rejection in two days.

"Do you know how long I've waited to hear you say that?" He leaned forward and pressed their foreheads together. His hands trembled as he cupped her face and then kissed her with all the love he felt in his heart. "Are we really going to do this? For real this time?"

Sofia pulled her hands from his grip and then threw her arms around his neck. "Yes! I love you so much." She leaned up on her toes and kissed him with every ounce of love and passion that was in her body. She gave and received so much that her whole body trembled like the last autumn leaf blowing in the wind.

When they both had to come up for air, Sofia held him tight while Ramell whispered against her hair. "I love you so much."

"I love you, too." Relief rushed through her like a tidal wave.

"I want to marry you," he said. "The right way. With family and friends around us to celebrate and witness our love."

Sofia laughed and cried at the same time. "I'll marry you anywhere, anytime."

"Harrumph."

Sofia and Ramell pulled apart to see Jacob standing nearby, smiling.

"I hate to interrupt but the photographer is waiting." He winked and then walked off.

Sofia and Ramell stole another kiss before they reluctantly pulled apart. "I guess we better get back to the wedding," she said.

"Save a dance for me?" he asked.

"I'll save all of them for you."

Thirty minutes later, everyone was in their places and watching Rachel float down the aisle. Sofia had never seen her sister look more beautiful. When she met Ethan in front of the minister and linked their hands, everyone sighed at just how beautiful the couple was together. When it came time to recite their vows, Ethan choked up a bit and every woman's heart swooned.

"I now pronounce you man and wife. You may now kiss the bride."

Ethan stepped forward and drew his wife into his arms, made a dramatic dip and then kissed Rachel passionately. While the wedding party cheered, Sofia and Ramell's gazes found one another. There was so much love in his eyes, Sofia could drown in it.

At the wedding reception, Ramell swept her into his arms and pressed their cheeks together. Sofia still struggled to keep her tears at bay when she reflected on just how close she came to losing the best thing that had ever happened to her.

"No tears," Ramell said, kissing their salty tracks.

Sofia smiled. "Don't worry. They're happy tears."

"Yeah?" He smiled. "Then those might be all right."

They floated around the dance floor, sharing Rachel and Ethan's special day and feeling like it was truly the beginning for them, as well. In a lot of ways, that was exactly what it was.

The beginning of happily ever after.

Epilogue

A year later...

Sofia sat on the edge of the doctor's table with her cell phone tucked under her ear while her fingers raced across her new iPad as she fired off one contract counteroffer after another. "Sorry, Larry, but that's not going to happen. You've only locked down Mary Bell for one season of *Paging the Doctor*. She's a big hit. The fans love her. If you want to lock her down for another four years then you're going to have come up with a figure that doesn't insult my intelligence." She only half listened to Larry Franklin's response because she knew that this was the part when studios started crying broke.

"Larry, if you feel that way then we can just let the contract run out and I can dedicate more attention to the numerous *movie* offers that have been flooding my in-box."

"Damn, Sofia. There you go beating me up again. I hoped that you becoming a mother was going to soften you up a bit."

"Are you kidding? Not with these hormones."

Larry laughed. "All right. All right. I can go up another ten percent. But that's it."

That managed to put a smile on her face. "I'll confer with my client and get back with you," she said noncommittally and then disconnected the call. But then her phone started ringing again. She was about to answer when Dr. Perry's voice startled her.

"You think you can fit in time in for your checkup?"

Sofia jumped and then flashed him an apologetic smile. "Sorry about that." She quickly put her phone on vibrate and sat it and her iPad down.

Ramell unfolded his arms and grabbed his wife's electronic gadgets. "Yes, please forgive my wife. She gets a little carried away sometimes."

Sofia glanced over at him. "Hey, I'm doing better. I've cut my work hours in half and only work three days a week."

"And I appreciate that, baby." He leaned over and kissed her before returning his attention to their doctor. "So what's the news doctor?"

Dr. Perry smiled at the loving couple. "I'm going to ask once again. Are you two sure that you want to know the sex of the baby?"

Sofia and Ramell smiled as their arms drifted around each other's waists.

"We're sure," Sofia said, giddy.

"All right. Then just lay back and let's get you hooked up."

Minutes later with her belly jelled down, Sofia and Ramell stared at the sonogram monitor in awe. When Dr. Perry pointed out the tiny little head and feet of their child, tears rushed their eyes as more love filled their hearts.

"Oh my God, baby. Look." Sofia reached for Ram's hand. "That's our baby."

"It sure is." Ram nodded and then planted a kiss against her forehead.

Dr. Perry pointed at the screen. "And this here tells me that you two are about to have…a boy."

Ramell dropped his wife's hand and pumped his fist high into the air. "Yeah! Yeah, baby!"

With tears streaming down her face, Sofia laughed at her husband's antics and then beamed when he then wrapped his arms around her and smothered her with kisses. "I take it that you're happy?"

"Are you kidding me? You've made me the happiest man in the world."

She smiled as she cupped his handsome face in her hands. "And you've made me the happiest woman. I love you."

"I've loved you for a gazillion years," he said tenderly.

"And I'll love you for a gazillion more," Sofia whispered, and sealed that promise with a kiss.

* * * * *

L♥VE IN THE LIMELIGHT

Fantasy, Fame and Fortune...Hollywood-Style!

Book #1
By *New York Times* and *USA TODAY*
Bestselling Author Brenda Jackson
STAR OF HIS HEART
August 2010

Book #2
By A.C. Arthur
SING YOUR PLEASURE
September 2010

Book #3
By Ann Christopher
SEDUCED ON THE RED CARPET
October 2010

Book #4
By *Essence* Bestselling Author Adrianne Byrd
LOVERS PREMIERE
November 2010

*Set in Hollywood's entertainment industry,
two unstoppable sisters and their two friends
find romance, glamour and dreams-come-true.*

REQUEST YOUR FREE BOOKS!

2 FREE NOVELS
PLUS 2 **FREE GIFTS!**

KIMANI™
ROMANCE

Love's ultimate destination!

KROM10R

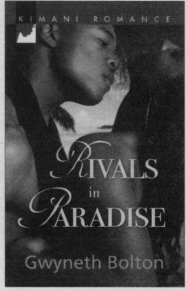

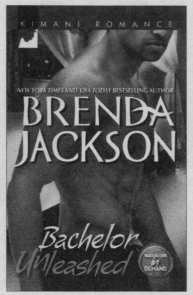